chouboli
and other stories
volume II

chouboli
and other stories
volume II

translated from the rajasthani
by christi a merrill, with kailash kabir

vijaydan

detha

FORDHAM ❋ UNIVERSITY ❋ PRESS

contents

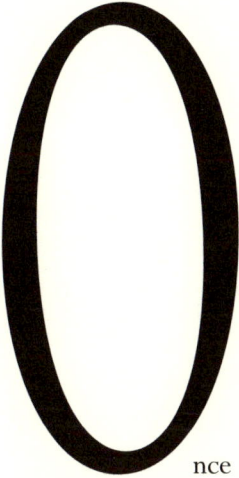

Once upon a time there was a heron who would go to the jawar field every day to take his fill of grain. Every day his mate would warn him that the soul of the farmer was very cruel, there was no mercy at all in his heart. If that nikuch ever caught hold of you he would certainly kill you. Listen to what I say, leave this field and find another place. But the heron did not heed her advice. And in the end it happened just the way the heron's mate had said it would. That miserable farmer went about coating the jawar plants with sweet, sticky chashni. When the heron came to pick grain, he got stuck right where he landed, and the farmer was waiting hidden in the jawar. As soon as he saw that the heron was stuck, he sprang out to catch him. The heron opened his beak wide to call out, and all the grain slipped from his beak.

The farmer put him under a basket at the edge of the field. The heron's mate waited for him until sunset – if the heron were free then surely he would have come. Their chicks began crying out in hunger. In the end the heron's mate comforted her chicks and flew off in search of her heron. She flew and flew and reached that very field of jawar. She saw the heron trapped under the basket and said:

> I warned you myself, I told you myself
>
> Don't pick the jawar in that field my love.

The heron answered:

> I'm alive I'm awake
>
> Fly my love right back to our chicks.

When she heard this, the heron's mate flew off. She reached her chicks and looked after them. But without her mate her soul would not be quenched. She comforted the chicks and then flew back to her heron. She flew around the entire field calling and calling. She didn't see the farmer, nor the basket on the edge of the field, nor did she sight her heron. At last she flew in the direction of the farmer's hut. She flew and flew and finally reached his hut. The farmer was inside the pen plucking the heron's feathers. The ground was littered with feathers white as can be. The heron had lost all colour and stood there silently. When she saw the straits he was in, tears starting falling from her eyes. Crying she called out:

> I warned you myself, I told you myself
>
> Don't pick the jawar in that field my love.

The heron answered:

I'm alive I'm awake

Fly my love right back to our chicks.

When she heard this, the heron's mate flew off. She reached her chicks and looked after them. But without her mate her soul would not be quenched. She comforted the chicks and then flew back to her heron. And what did she see but that her mate had been cut into pieces and kept in an iron bowl. The ground was littered with feathers white as can be while inside the bowl sat a pile of meat glistening red. The heron's mate began sobbing and weeping bitterly, tears streaming from her eyes. She cried:

I warned you myself, I told you myself

Don't pick the jawar in that field my love.

The heron answered:

I'm alive I'm awake

Fly my love right back to our chicks.

When she heard this, the heron's mate flew off. She reached her chicks and looked after them. She offered her beak to them and cried. But without her mate her soul would not be quenched. She comforted her chicks and then flew back to her heron. What did she see but the farmer stirring a big clay handi pot, under which a fire had been set, in which the heron was cooking. The heron's mate began sobbing and weeping bitterly, tears streaming from her eyes. She cried:

I warned you myself, I told you myself

Don't pick the jawar in that field my love.

The heron boiling and bubbling inside the handi answered:

I'm alive I'm awake

Fly my love right back to our chicks.

When she heard this, the heron's mate flew off. She reached her chicks and looked after them. She offered her beak to them and cried. But without her mate her soul would not be quenched. She comforted the chicks and then flew back to her heron. What did she see but the handi lying empty in the outer aangan of the estate. The farmer had eaten his fill and was washing up. The heron's mate began sobbing and weeping bitterly, tears streaming from her eyes. She cried:

> I warned you myself, I told you myself
>
> Don't pick the jawar in that field my love.

The heron, half-digested inside the farmer's stomach, answered:

> I'm alive I'm awake
>
> Fly my love right back to our chicks.

But without her mate her soul would not be quenched. She alighted on the edge of the roof and there she sat.

The farmer was surprised that the heron was still alive and awake. He started worrying how he was going to digest this live heron. He ran to his wife and said, "There's a heron in my stomach that's still alive, I'm going to vomit him up. You get the big lathi and stand next to me. As soon as he comes out of my mouth, hit him as hard as you can. Then I'll cook the heron again and eat him. Now stand here like this with the lathi held directly overhead, and as soon as his beak appears, hit him right square on his most sensitive point. Don't let that heron get away!"

Both husband and wife took their places in the aangan. The wife stood on tip-toes fully alert, lathi in hand. Her husband started to vomit. With the vomit out came the heron fluttering his wings and flew off. The wife swung the lathi with all her might and caught her husband full in the mouth. Thirty-two teeth white as can be all fell out. Blood glistening red started streaming from his mouth. He passed out and fell to the ground with a loud ta-dakh.

The heron's mate flew with her heron up into the heavens. They returned home to their chicks, wings gleaming white as snow. Pearls of joy streaming from their eyes rained down so thick they covered the earth in a layer of glimmering white.

cannibal

I t so often happens that the descendants of Adam manifest basic natures other than those of man. A person might well remind you of certain flora or fauna – for instance, an aak, thornapple, prickly-pear, or acacia, or even a vulture, jackal, python, donkey or lion. And so it was once that a temple priest took birth in a woman's womb sown with a man's seed. But he appeared instead to be a cross between a dhatura cactus and a crow.

He was but a child when his parents had grown so weary of his wicked deeds that they sent him away to the temple of the goddess hoping he would reform in her care. But feed a cactus milk and butter everyday, and it will still be just a cactus. A crow can spend years listening to hymns and bhajans, and still squawk like a crow. Every being has a certain nature that becomes evident right from birth and stays with him until death. A donkey can spend his entire life reading from the sacred Bhagvad Gita, and still he'll be nothing but a donkey. This brahmin wasted plenty of sandalwood paste anointing himself. He chanted his mala. Offered puja to the goddess. Partook of bhang. And ganja. His eyes glowed red as cinders, day and night. Thick lips. Yellowed teeth. Beard down to his belly, hair matted and twisted in jata as tangled as a weaver bird's nest. Towering height. Stumpy neck. Body covered in fur like a bear.

Fortunately for this worthless brahmin, his wife was simple and meek. And yet he beat her whenever he felt like it, as if wife-beating was part of his daily routine. She consoled herself with the thought that maybe getting beaten up by the husband was part of domestic life. It was only when there was no food left to cook that she began to worry. It wasn't easy surviving on the meagre daily offerings made to the goddess of their temple. And with the brahmin being what he was, faith in the goddess gradually dwindled. Offerings grew smaller day by day. Even the goddess began to worry.

One day after dinner the brahmin had just smoked some ganja and was on his way to bed when he said to his wife, "This goddess of ours is a cheap whore. What khak faith is anyone going to have in her when her own priest is this poor? Doing all this puja-paath has made me useless. I'm good for nothing else now. Makes me so mad I've got a mind to go over to the temple and send her and myself up in flames. I'll wait a few days and then you just watch, I'm really going to teach her a lesson."

"Don't leave me behind like that!" his wife cried out, "How will I ever survive in this world alone, without husband or goddess to rely on?"

"Oh, I didn't think about that. Good thing you spoke up. Fine. Let's wait until the next new moon then to pull our stunt. People will be talking about it for years!"

He sat down on the edge of the bed. His wife exclaimed, "This can't be happening! How are you going to fall asleep when you haven't beaten me yet?"

Now in his childhood the brahmin may have forgotten himself and smiled once or twice, but even if the word laughter had crossed his lips ever since, he had no memory of it. But tonight when he heard his wife's words, a faint grin flickered on his lips for the very first time. "You need a good thrashing to relax, hunh? You probably think this is strange, but it's only when I'm beating you up that I too feel like I am a man. And you are the only one in the world I can flex my strength against. I suppose if we had children, I'd knock them about too. You know the pleasure of displaying your might is no small pleasure. Even so, you might miss these thrashings as much as your mother's house, but I've had enough. From now on, if I lay my hands on anyone, it's going to be to wring that damn goddess's neck. I'll find myself a hammer and go in there and smash her to pieces. Then I'll set the whole temple on fire with me inside and die in peace. Look, if I forget, make sure you remind me. We can't let the next new moon go by."

The brahmin slept well for the first time in ages. But his wife couldn't close her eyes once. How had this burden suddenly been dumped onto her shoulders? Obey her husband, and there'd be disaster. Disobey him, disaster. When had they ever seen even a glimmer of happiness in this life? Nothing but grief and misery. Good thing they didn't have children. They'd just spend all their time crying over their fate. Troubles turned and churned inside her head until it felt absolutely empty – no more worries, no more sorrows. How many shades of pleasure and pain, joy and despair are hidden in the black cloak of night? That even Vidhata the Creator does not know.

Well, time doesn't heed even an apocalypse, so why would it concern itself with this measly brahmin priest? The cycle of days and nights moved along at their natural pace, and finally the new moon came. The goddess was upset. There was no telling what that troublemaker would do! If the worshippers' faith in her lapsed for a moment, there would be none left even to say her name. Other creatures in the world thought of nothing but saving their own hides. It wouldn't matter to them if the Creator died today or tomorrow – vultures, crows, jackals and ants wouldn't leave even His corpse alone. If she had to leave this temple, she wouldn't find another for a hundred kos in any direction. There's no relying on these selfish humans! You never knew how and when their needs and motives would shift.

The brahmin's wife told herself that once in her life she might as well do something out of the ordinary. She reminded her husband of his resolve the night before the new moon.

He threw a fit. "You fool! You're reminding me just as I'm falling asleep?! Tell me first thing tomorrow morning."

But the next morning when the brahmin was setting off for the temple, his wife's mind was on other matters and she forgot. This made him even angrier. "How many times did I tell you to remind me, and still you forgot! If I had relied on you, this whole plan would have been as good as cow dung! I'm going to borrow a hammer from someone today and arrange for the wood and kindling. You come with me after dinner tonight. The whole region will be talking about us tomorrow."

Meanwhile, the goddess was in a state. She couldn't concentrate on the aarti being offered. She knew her brahmin too well. He could get into one of his moods anytime now and smash her to pieces. It was in her best interest to think of a way to appease him.

The sun was setting as he was performing the last evening rites when suddenly the goddess emerged from her idol. Adorned from head to toe in priceless jewels and glittering diamonds, she sparkled like a thousand lamps. When the brahmin looked up and saw this lone devotee standing beside him, he thought this was his golden opportunity. He was just about to snatch away her jewellery when she spoke: "Son, I have been testing you all these years. If only you had waited a little longer, you would have received the very throne of Indra. But you have lost patience prematurely. Nevertheless, I will give you whatever you ask for."

The temple cymbals tumbled from his hands, sending piercing clangs echoing through the small temple alcove. The goddess stood before him smiling. He swallowed nervously and asked, "And what if I had died first?"

She kept smiling and reassured him, "I would never have let that happen. Our devotees receive our unfailing care. It was simply due to an oversight in the divine realm that your evaluation has been delayed so long."

And what if she disappeared just as suddenly as she had appeared? There was no telling with these goddesses! So he promptly said, "Give me all your jewellery then. Then we'll both get to enjoy the life of leisure."

"But I'd be lost without my jewellery. Divine jewellery is useless for you mortals. It would turn to sand at your touch."

"So why did you say you'd give me whatever I asked for? I asked for what I wanted. And unlike you, I mean what I say when I say it. Well, at least now I know; next time I need anything I'll just get myself a hammer. Hunh! Anyway, there's no hiding my troubles from you. If you really want to grant me a boon, then just go ahead and do so. Give me anything you want."

Such bravado! She could scarcely conceal her rage. She knew this worshipper well. He had suffered too much to be easily cowed. A man living a cushy life could never hazard such recklessness. But the brahmin would get soft too, as soon as he tasted luxury. Then she wouldn't have to worry. This was the kind of man who'd lop off his nose just to be an awful sight for others. So she'd give him a boon that would please him, yes, but do more for those around him. That would make him burn with envy. She said: "All these years you have spent worshipping me, and still your soul hasn't come clean. I am ashamed just to be associated with you. Get rid of that fire burning in your heart. Whenever it flares up, try doing something helpful for someone instead."

Listening to advice about helping others only made him sick. "What kind of talk is this now? I know all this already. So stop your sermonizing and just give me my boon."

"You are truly one in a million. I am impressed by your impudence. Of what use are all those fawning fools to me, constantly grovelling and begging? And here you can't even look after your own interest. From now on, I will look after you."

"Fine. But if you've come up with such a grand idea, what's taking you so long?"

The goddess was in such a benevolent mood that day she didn't even mind such insolence. She laughed and said, "All children are equal in a mother's eyes. Maternal feelings are never lacking, even for the most wicked. Until this day, no one has ever received a boon such as the one I am about to grant you. And along with you others will profit too."

"Others will profit? By *my* boon? What could be worse! I have no use for a boon like that."

"You have spent your entire life enduring one hardship after another. It has distorted your thinking a little. Getting angry like this won't help. Go. From now on, anything you ask for you shall get. But whatever you ask for others will get too, and twice as much, for twelve and twelve makes twenty four kos around."

"You call that a boon?! It's worse than a curse! Compared to this boon of yours, my miserable life is a hundred-thousand times better. Take back your stupid boon and leave me alone!"

No sooner had he uttered the words than the goddess vanished as miraculously as she had appeared. He began shaking her idol in fury, but not a sound came from the stone, nor a tiny flicker. He stood there awhile completely still. Then he thought to himself, I'll just go home and talk it over with the wife. How could it hurt? After all these years, finally the goddess had granted him a boon!

He felt happy as he walked home from the temple. His wife was standing in the doorway. Such long, bounding strides! She had never seen him like this. She called out, "What happened? Why the rush?"

"Today I found out that you never waste words on someone used to kicks."

Then the brahmin narrated in detail all that had led up to his receiving the boon. It was as if all the suffering she had endured all these years had never been. Her happiness knew no bounds. She told him, "I always knew, all the time that you spent in puja would one day prove worthwhile."

"Prove worthwhile? What do you mean? Whatever I get everyone else will get too, only twice as much. You couldn't think of a worse curse! Have you been drinking bhang?!"

"As a woman I have no right to offer you advice, but really, what does it matter to us if others have more? We have spent so much of our lives toiling in such misery, just the thought of it makes my hair stand on end. Let's just try to be happy. Then we'll know. It's up to you now. What's there to worry about? I bound my fortunes to your destitute ways. Why can't you grant me just this one glimpse of joy?"

He was not a man born with compassion in his heart. So it was no small matter that he did not start thrashing her in fury after hearing his wife's nonsense. He scratched his head and said, "You are right. We should see if it works. After all, the goddess may be trying to trick us somehow."

But what should he ask for first? Suddenly he thought of his broken pipe and empty bowl of ganja. He called out, "Oh Mother Goddess, if this boon is true, then give me a new pipe and a big bowl of ganja."

The words had scarcely left his lips when the gifts appeared. They stared wide-eyed, flabbergasted, still as statues. If their every wish would come true this easily, there would be no end to their joy! Every want of the past would be taken care of. And what did he wish for first – just a pipe and some ganja. But what now? And what if the boon was only meant to be used once, then what would he do? That would be an outrage. And everyone else getting twice as much? What torture! This was a real dilemma. Maybe if he could just have some of that fresh ganja, his mind would clear a little. He tamped the ganja into the pipe till it was full, and his wife brought him an ember to light it with. He was thinking about what to wish for next. They had spent all their lives scraping by. Now what would be the best thing to wish for next, this or that, that or this? His mind was tangled up in knots. He thought of so many things to wish for. This was the kind of leisure afforded by a full stomach. One who goes hungry is not even allowed the luxury of clear thinking. His wife wouldn't stop nagging him. So to please her he wished for a canister of flour, a container of salt, a bin full of pepper and spices, and a bundle of firewood. It was odd – one moment he asked for things, the next moment there they were before him.

The couple was astounded. His wife dashed off to light the fire. Why linger now? As happy as he was, he was still bothered. Everyone around him was getting twice as much. Nothing could be worse!

The brahmin's wife fed her husband and then sat down to eat. There's nothing like the pleasure of a full stomach. For the first time in the brahmin's life, he had eaten his fill, and it only made him sadder. He went to his wife and said, "Dear, would you please do me one favour?"

"Have I ever refused that you suddenly have to start asking?"

"Refuse, and you'd have had me to answer to. I'd have paddled you with my shoe so hard you'd lose every hair on your head. Now go look in every house and see if they've got twice as much as we have."

"Why should we bother with anyone else? Now we don't even have to beg for a light. And it is because of you that everyone is prospering. And others are benefitting no less than us."

"Completely brainless, and still you go on chattering like you have something to say. I've stood up under the winds of unhappiness for all these years, but just this little gust of happiness has knocked me flat inside of a day. If everyone is doing well just because of me, then I might as well die. Don't argue with me, just do as I say!"

What more could she say? She spun around the village like an unwound top. Wherever she went she found the goddess's words had come true. And in every house it was the same. People were dumbfounded. Was this some sort of magic or sorcery? Then the brahmin's wife told them about the boon. At last her husband's penance had been rewarded.

When she came home she found her husband sitting outside with a long face. At the sound of her footsteps he lifted his head and asked, "Is it true? Are they getting twice as much as we are?"

When the pujarin said Yes, it was as if a cannon had been fired into his ear. He wasn't worried about all those he didn't know, but the thought of the people in his own village getting all those things made him crazy. And not one speck of thanks – the bastards hadn't said a word. Helping ingrates like these should be considered a sin! He reeled around like a mad man and collapsed on his broken cot. His wife started massaging his hands and feet.

After a time she tried to soothe him by saying, "Why are you getting so upset over nothing? Let the world go up in smoke. What do you care?"

"How am I supposed to let it all go up in smoke? If it really did, I would be content."

"The world exists only as long as you have breath. Take care of yourself and everything else will be fine. Look in the mirror. You used to be so healthy. You've grown skinny as a thorny bush right before my eyes. If I had a lump of gur, a pot of butter, and a kilo of fenugreek seeds, I would make you laddus, and then feed you some halwa with dinner. First get back your strength. Then you can do whatever you want."

As soon as he heard the words laddu and halwa the brahmin's mouth began to water. He would have to get back his strength first if he wanted to deal with these people properly. No one knows when he would take his last breath. It's not like the Lord of Death trumpets his arrival. First I'll let myself get better, he thought, then I'll deal with everyone one by one. He lay down and wished for the list of things his wife had asked for. They appeared as soon as he said the words. He cooled down just at the smell of the ghee.

The brahmin's wife felt as if she'd been given ten lives all at once. First she looked at the lump of jaggery, then at the pot of ghee. In a house where even salt had been scarce once, this was the greatest luxury imaginable. After a time she resurfaced from her pool of happiness and asked, "Am I to cook these things in my bare hands? I need a skillet and some nice bronze utensils."

Surprisingly enough, the brahmin went along with it. The skillet and pots and pans appeared before her in an instant. It would take her no time to cook some halwa.

The brahmin swallowed a mouthful of delicious hot halwa. Then he turned to his wife and asked her earnestly, "I'm not dreaming, am I? Are my eyes open? Look at me carefully."

"First you tell me, are my eyes open?"

"Yes, they're wide open. You look awake to me."

"And your eyes are open. You are wide awake. Today we made halwa on our own hearth! Things we couldn't even dream about till yesterday today we're seeing with our own eyes."

Without their being aware of it, a longing for happiness had begun to blossom in their hearts. Before today, they had endured the worst of hardships, the hardest of trials. Now they needed to drink in all the happiness they could bear. The rest of the world faded away.

Twilight came and the star-studded night descended to earth, with the chirping, singing birds its jingling anklets. What a miracle the stars were to behold! Such gentle darkness! Such a soft, caressing breeze! How beautiful the world looked now that they were happy. Now that they had this boon, why should anything be out of their grasp? The brahmin's contentment twinkled among the stars. At that moment, he was blissfully unaware of anyone else's sorrow or joy.

He looked at his wife and said, "If only we had some cows and a water buffalo, how would that be? Yoghurt and cream right there whenever you wanted."

"If we don't even have a proper house to live in, what good are cows and buffaloes? Besides a nice meadow, we'd also need a pen and a barn to store fodder. Then we would be set."

"With a boon like this, why just scrape by? We can live as we please!"

Suddenly a thought flashed through the brahmin's mind like a spark. "What do you say we use this boon to play a trick on the goddess? Of course, she can go around bringing us all these petty little household things. But what if we wish for something really spectacular? She'd bow down before me begging to take back her words. When I was young, my grandmother used to tell me a story of a legendary palace, a palace made of gold! With a boon like this, why should I keep grovelling before her like a beggar? Even seven generations of goddesses would have trouble building a palace of gold. And if she can't keep her promise, that would make her look bad, wouldn't it?"

He joined his hands and made a playful wish, "O Mother, O Revered One, if you are truly as good as your word, grant my wish for a palace of gold, full of goldenware to match."

No sooner had the words left his mouth than his golden palace sprung up around him. He felt as if he had suddenly risen up in the air as he lay there.

The loose weave of his cot rose up taut and rigid under his back. Even his cot had turned to gold! He sat up, flabbergasted. Instead of his crumbling walls plastered with cow dung, the walls shone bright yellow. He rubbed his eyes and looked again. Had his impossible wish really come true? His wife was standing nearby, gaping in astonishment. What divine leela was this?

She lit a golden lamp. They both stood next to the walls feeling them and admiring their lustre. How could the goddess be capable of this? He told his wife, "If only we had asked for this straight away! She can double things like salt and cooking oil, but I'd like to see her make a pair of golden palaces!"

The brahmin's wife looked in the cupboards and found two or three of her husband's pipes – of gold. Ah! Even the old clay ganja pot had turned to gold! The brahmin filled his pipe and began to smoke. Then he had a coughing fit that lasted a while. He was getting old. If the goddess had only come to her senses twenty years earlier, then his life would have been worth living. But how much longer did they have to enjoy such a palace? How many more nights, how many more dreams? The irony of receiving such a boon so late in life made it an agony rather than a blessing. What was the use of a heavy monsoon shower when the crops had already withered and died?

The brahmin looked at his wife and said, "You've turned into an old woman. A person should be youthful and fit to live in such a palace."

"You're worse off than I am. Don't start worrying about me. All I want is to leave this earth before you. I ask for nothing more. I've seen the Golden Palace with my own eyes, what more could I want? Ai, I have an idea. Can't the goddess make us young again?"

"Arre, of course, why not? What's happening to my mind! Well, never mind. Better late than never."

The moment he asked the goddess for them to be young again, their youth was restored instantly. It would have been difficult for one to even dream up such a leela, and here they were both living it! Could anyone have ever known such unparalleled joy? They were so incredulous with happiness they never even thought of enjoying the pleasures their youthful bodies were capable of. The blissful night passed in the wink of an eye.

The brahmin awoke at the first light of dawn. "Does the sun rise any differently on a day like today?" he wondered.

He climbed his golden staircase to the golden roof. All around he could see nothing but golden palaces. As if countless suns had climbed over the horizon. Flames of jealousy started raging in his heart. He squinted in their brilliant light. Everyone else had two golden palaces while he only had one! And it was all due to him. He could gladly suffer all the misery and pain in the world, but the thought that he alone was responsible for the happiness of others – this was more than he could take. What fate could be worse?

He felt trapped in a treacherous maze. The flames in his heart rose so high and fierce they would have scorched the sun. The beasts in him that were his nature – the jackal, crow, tiger and snake – ran amok. He started running around in circles barking like a rabid dog. "May one of my eyes go blind! May one of my eardrums tear! May a bottomless well be dug in front of my palace!"

The words were barely out of his mouth than his wife shrieked, "Oh Lord, what's happening? Did our fabulous palace disappear? Has the rising sun descended back into the earth?"

He understood at once. His feet thudded down the golden stairs as he ran to her. His wife was feeling her way along the wall with her hands outstretched before her and was just at the doorway when he started shouting as loud as he could, "Stop! Stop right there! Don't take another step! There's a deep well right in front of you!"

But the brahmin's wife couldn't hear a word he said. She tumbled over the edge just as he leapt from the last step. He heard the splash far below. His life partner had abandoned him just when he had come into his prime.

After that he wandered through each and every house in each and every village within twelve and twelve makes twenty-four kos. As he entered each village he would look around with his one good eye and see people tumbling into their wells one by one. Before long, they were all finished. He cackled like a demon. So pleased with their pair of golden palaces that they walked straight into Death's lap!

Now he was the sole proprietor of all these golden palaces. There was no one left to dispute his claim. Each night he slept in a different palace. There was no one left to receive twice as much as him. So what if the goddess had given him a boon? He had enough brains in his head to know how to use the boon. And so the goddess's boon had at last been vanquished. He jumped in glee, threw his arms up in the air and admired all his golden palaces with his good eye. Too bad there was no one to witness his supreme joy.

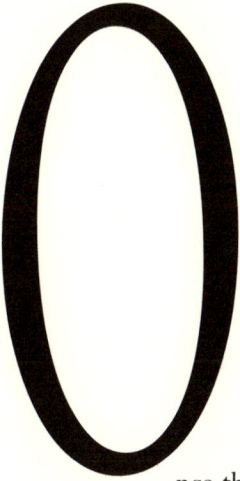

Once there was a king as just as he was generous. Under his rule subjects enjoyed complete freedom in choosing their punishment. Criminals would weigh their options carefully and select a punishment they deemed best. Once a thief was asked to choose between two punishments for thieving. He could eat one hundred large onions or, if he wished, he could receive one hundred shoe lashings. Now, this one was a thief among thieves. Rather than suffer any demeaning shoe lashings, he would gladly toss back a hundred onions.

The justice-loving king smiled and said, "As you wish."

But the reality of the thief's wish was not all he'd bargained for. He had only eaten four or five onions when he felt as if his mouth was full of flames. Tears started flowing from his eyes. He couldn't eat any more onions — just the sight made him want to vomit. But he had to fulfill his punishment one way or another. So he gladly chose to receive the shoe lashings instead. He was a thief after all — quite accustomed to being beaten by shoes. At least he'd no longer have that terrible burning in his mouth! His head might start throbbing but it could take care of itself. Why was the royal executioner taking so long? Old crusty shoes started raining down on his bare head until everything went black. His head had turned completely numb. If he let them beat his head with a hundred shoes there'd be no head left to speak of! He'd hardly taken twenty shoe lashings so far and already his head had swelled up like a syrup-soaked malpua. Eating onions was better in comparison. His head was ringing so hard from the shoe lashings that he'd forgotten all about the burning in his mouth. He cried out in agony for the executioner to stop. He begged the king with folded hands to be allowed to finish the rest of the onions.

The raja was a just ruler and so didn't like to force anyone to do anything against their wishes. The thief's throbbing head hadn't even cleared when he stepped up to the pile of onions and began eating away. But as soon as the ache in his head subsided he began to feel the stinging in his mouth hot as live coals. His eyes burned and watered as viciously as before. He rubbed them with his hands and the stinging only grew worse. It took all his courage and will to swallow twenty, twenty five more, but then he had to give up — the burning in his eyes, nose and mouth was so bad he forgot how bad the shoes were. Being thrashed by shoes was so much better! He had the full freedom to choose his punishment. Pleading, he begged to be beaten with the remaining shoes.

The generous raja granted his request at once. The executioner stood by clutching a pair of shoes. The thief bowed his head and the beating started once more. He gritted his teeth against the pain, but when they reached sixty he thought his head would break into little pieces if he took even one more lash. He clasped his hands once more and cried and begged, "I have no courage left to endure even the sight of another shoe. I'm ready to eat the rest of the onions."

He began eating the onions, rubbing his poor swollen head all the while. At least his poor head was intact! Eating the onions finally made the pains in his head diminish. But that flame in his mouth started glowing again. The nausea started welling up again. If he ate one more onion the life in him would surely flee. He was ready once again for the shoes. But where would he find it in himself to stand up to that throbbing pain? After twenty shoes the burning in his mouth cooled off. One way or another, he would just have to eat the rest of the onions and end his misery.

But his misery lasted exactly as long as it was meant to last. Going back and forth according to his wishes, he ate all hundred onions, and also suffered all one hundred shoe lashings. Then why didn't he simply rally the strength to endure one form of punishment throughout? But who could ever explain the meaning of such helplessness?

the limit

Stories, like clouds, rain and moonlight never grow old. Even when they have been in existence for countless years, each day they seem new. This story begins with a seth who lived in a village nestling somewhere between light and dark. He had in his cellar riches beyond count, glimmering like the stars on a moonless night. It was as if the guards of all the Seven Joys themselves stood in his aangan ready to attend on him. His wife was Goddess Lakshmi incarnate. He had five sons, all healthy, virtuous and dutiful. All were married, to bahus both beautiful and modest. He had two apsara-like daughters who had been joined in matrimony to homes of equal standing.

Their wealth ran like water day and night without ever diminishing, the waters of happiness spilling over day after day without ever nearing shallow. Of all the eighty four lakh forms of life a being could assume, a human manifestation was surely the best! And not only that, but to be born into such happiness, such unimaginable wealth! So glorious, like another moon in the sky. Even the king envied him his riches. So filled was he with wealth's intoxicating powers, the seth believed that the day itself rose and fell with the lid of his eye.

One could say that the seth was charitable by nature. One could also say that his speculations on his next birth led his hand to be that much more open in this one. He granted every wish of the poor and wretched. He simply did not know how to turn anyone down.

One day the raja called him to court. He invited the seth to sit right there on the throne with him and then began, "O Seth, if there remains in this kingdom a single beggar, the offence shall fall on your name. If anyone should die of hunger, it would be a disgrace to your wealth. Have you ever stopped to think about this?"

The seth smiled faintly. "O Annadaata, why do you mock me? If other than Bhagwan, not even His Highness has it in his power to control such things, then why put the blame on a worthless baniya like myself? It will be wrong if I heed your words and worse if I don't. Better I should rid myself of these wicked ears. O Protector of the Poor, I would rather step into a noose than be taunted like this."

Truth be told, the royal treasury was running a little low. The king was buttering him up expressly to ingratiate himself with the seth. He was able to force out such flattery only with effort. Otherwise such words would never cross a king's lips. And when they did, even swords and cannons could not compare with their might. The seth had become so relaxed the raja decided he could ask for an even heftier loan. Indeed, to have a raja in one's debt was a chance in a lakh! Both were pleased.

For the first time in his life the seth felt true pride in his wealth. Today he had overshadowed even the mountain! What greater happiness could there be on this earth?

As he was riding home to his haveli in his sixteen-horse golden chariot, it seemed as if all the world had turned out at his nod. Nature herself rushed to comply with his wishes like a common ploughman or labourer waiting expectantly for his command. At his whim the breeze blew, the clouds rumbled, lightning flashed, the rains poured down, the greenery unfurled, and at his whim the sun and the moon rose in turn.

He arrived at his haveli fast as the wind. There were more people gathered at the gate than anyone could possibly count. As his chariot parted the crowds like the waters of the sea, their loud cheers – Jaya! Jaya! – rent the sky. So many open palms swimming before his eyes, like fish come to feed at this opportune moment of a solar eclipse. They had more faith in his charity than in the raja's or even Bhagwan himself. These two hands were capable of such feats, these outstretched hands beyond count believed in them. He gazed at the sun and watched it be swallowed up by darkness. Where were its rays? Where its lifegiving light? What happened to the radiant sun? What Maya had transformed it into this black iron circle of a skillet? Must be that the sun itself had bowed before his greater glory!

At last by his mercy the sun edged free. The darkness began to lift at the rim. Sunlight began to pour down on earth once again to great cheers. The shouts were even louder than before. Every particle and mote was bathed in light. Goodness, how could so much light have ever been kept hidden?! And so completely that not a single ray could gleam through!

He had no way of knowing just how miraculous he was. Today his eyes shone with a new light. The glow of his smile suffused with the radiance of the sun as he went to the sethani and exclaimed, "Did you see the miraculous effects of my alms-giving? The word on everyone's lips is that the disaster befalling the sun was averted only through my grace."

His wife didn't say a word. She just smiled as she poured holy Ganga water from a golden pitcher for him to rinse his hands and face. He began to describe exactly what Rajaji had said to him and concluded, "What will happen to this world after I am gone? I've wracked my brain but still haven't found an answer."

She said, "Why are you wracking your brain over such inanities? A man's life or death doesn't make any difference to this world. Who knows how many like you have already slipped into the mouth of Kal without a trace? Rajas and emperors, sages and seers have all come onto this earth and departed in their time. No one's death has ever brought anything to a halt. Only Bhagwan knows what is and what is meant to be. Life lacks lustre when clouded with such illusions."

The seth was stunned. He started stammering, "Illusion! How can this be illusion? You think that people won't be devastated by my death? That the sun and the moon will keep on rising and setting as they always have? That the breeze and the rain are so ungrateful they wouldn't even show this much courtesy to me? You think I'm lying?"

"I don't know about truth and lies. I was just speaking of illusion. Everyone is under this illusion. Lakhs of men die everyday. Is nature going to pay her respects to them all? Forget nature, even one's progeny perform the obligatory condolence rites and then forget about their mother and father. Life goes on. Yes, when you die everything ends. This world is only for the living. The only place for the dead is the cremation ground. Not even the cremation ground, for when you die even your body is left behind. You are unaware of the corpse, of the wood, the fire, the skeleton and the ashes. All these troubles are left to the living. Forget you and me, if Bhagwan himself were to cease to exist, nature's leela wouldn't stop for a moment. It wouldn't make any difference to a single petal."

Stars began to dance before his eyes. He wouldn't have imagined this even in a dream. How could he believe what was coming from the sethani's mouth? Believe her, and everything he'd had faith in until today would be destroyed. How to live without this faith, without this illusion? Even with all this wealth, death could not be averted? He wanted to say something as brilliant as the sun, but his tongue would not express it. He sat down on the edge of the bed, his eyes staring vacantly into hers, and said in a tone that sounded as if everything he had were lost, "You read the shastras day and night, and this is the truth you arrive at? Then what meaning is there in living? You have spent so many years churning that water, one would think at the very least you'd have come up with some butter. You plunged into those shastras and you didn't even find a leech. Your learning, my money, none of it is worth anything but a lump of dirt."

She spoke in a voice that sounded as if it were coming from a cave, "Yes, we've taken different roads and arrived at the same destination. My learning, your money, they are indeed all worthless. A grand illusion. I have journeyed past the limitless light of knowledge and arrived at infinite darkness. There is nothing beyond this darkness. Only death which glimmers in infinite darkness is immutable, everlasting: This is the first and the last truth. No matter how much pride man has in his learning, it is all just a mirage. A delusion borne of ignorance. But this delusion is more necessary for life than air and water."

To the seth such a vision was as good as a living death. He took the sethani by her arms and began shaking her, crying out as if pleading for alms, "Bas! Bas! Stop, I beg you, in the name of Bhagwan!"

He wasn't able to say another word. It was as if his lips had stuck together. He struggled to stay conscious. Darkness and more darkness in every direction. In the end he fell on the bed in a faint.

The sethani had been waiting for just such a moment all her life.

She'd been married years and years before when she was still a child. She was her mother's favourite, then was made a bride and went to live with her in-laws, like a bird finding sanctuary in the shade of another tree. Everyone at her parents' house had a passion for reading the shastras. So she brought with her in her dowry the Vedas, the Puranas, the Upanishads, the Six Philosophies, the *Gita*, the *Mahabharata*, the *Ramayana* and other such sacred tomes. Whenever she had a free moment she'd immerse herself in her reading. She always left the windows of her eyes and soul open. The touch of all those black letters only increased the light of her knowledge. And whether consciously or unconsciously, as time passed, the essence of these things began to appear before her beyond the letters on the page. Her in-laws were very pleased to have a bahu the very image of Goddess Saraswati. And as luck would have it, an Aghori guru came into her life and a fourth moon was added to the skies of her knowledge.

Already there were riches beyond measure in her in-laws' house. And then her husband was made heir to a childless uncle's fortunes. Countless wealth accumulated generation upon generation came to him without his lifting a little finger.

Then she had come to a most unusual resolve. She was sitting in the bridal chamber one evening, reading the *Sankhyakarika* by lamplight when she asked her husband, "If you don't mind, I have something to say to you."

He stroked her cheek and said, "I can't believe a word would ever come from your mouth that I couldn't accept. What did you want to tell me?"

"For several days now a thought has been hovering in my mind. We have each taken on a wager that is actually quite curious. Please listen to me carefully. You have wealth beyond measure, and still you are not at peace unless you are earning more and more. You spend all your intelligence and conviction making more and more money, as if you could arrive at that edge beyond which there is no more. As if there were no greater happiness or bliss beyond arriving at that limit of wealth. You keep marching down this road, and even when you don't arrive, you keep marching on. And I'm going along my own way, and even when I don't arrive, I keep going on. Towards that limit of knowledge and learning. Meanwhile, we don't enjoy even the name of rest, contentment, nor patience. All we have is that road, our feet and our will. We keep marching on and on – until we reach the real end."

That day, like now, neither could imagine abandoning the path they had set out on, nor taking a moment to stop. And that limit had not arrived, nor even a clear border. It seemed to draw near and then slide away. Time and time again they thought that the limit had arrived, but when they reached they realized there was no sign of it. This was just the way the mind worked. Or where would you ever find the end?

All those golden moments playing hide and seek with us have now joined Lord Kal. Like a sweet dream that has passed. Where did all those years go? Hidden beneath the day's sunny light or the dark ashes of night? Yesterday's new bride has become the mother of seven. The mother-in-law of five brides. Time past does not return, nor does youth. When they are gone, wealth and knowledge have the lure of a distant mountain, or the horizon. Thirst smoulders within you day and night. Sleeping or waking, it's always the same thirst. We have an abundance of wealth and knowledge. But it's all useless. Only when you do not have them do you know their true value and meaning. Heap on more than you need, and it may as well be sand. Knowledge works backwards. It tricks you like Sita's mrigtrishna for the ever elusive golden deer. This mirage of knowledge is the worst ignorance of all. False thirst for a false faith!

A little while later the seth woke up. He didn't know if an hour had passed or a year. It was as if he had emerged from the depths of a bottomless sea. As if a roiling river were flooding in his head. And with it who knows how much trash and debris. It seemed as if he had been given a new life. He rose from his bed with a groan. He began gazing at the sethani as if she were an acquaintance from years past or someone he was seeing for the first time.

His eyes and lips spoke together, "You've spent all your years running after knowledge. So tell me, if I realized today for the first time in my life that even with all this wealth and property I'm not happy, then what are other men living for? How do they find meaning in their lives? Why do people go around multiplying like fleas? No food to eat, no clothes to wear, no house to live in. For those unlucky enough, they must not even be able to dream of money. For them death is a great boon. Then why do they creep into the pus of neverending misery and suffering? It's better to die than to always have your palm outstretched, begging."

She came and sat next to him. She said, "You may or may not like the answer I must give, but I have to tell you in no uncertain terms that this is not the final truth. Only now have I begun to understand the hollowness of knowledge. Each one's understanding of happiness and sadness is different, depending on his worldview, and the people he is with. What you consider misery they don't see that way, which is why they can call living to get by happiness. Everyone takes pride in his own way of thinking. Everyone is satisfied with himself."

"That kind of satisfaction might as well be khak! Living to get by you might as well be roasting in hell! You can't die before your time comes. The poor things, what more can they do?"

"Here's something you can do! Go try wringing any poor, miserable person's neck and see! Tell me if he doesn't strangle you back. They have a far greater desire to live than we do. For them their biggest comfort lies in their desire for fleeting happiness. And they're no less satisfied by the thought that everyone leaves this earth empty-handed. No power matches that of death. Not the raja's, not the learned's, not the millionaire's. No one can take even a pebble away with them. In the court of death there's no difference between big and small — if the poor didn't keep this thought in mind, there'd be no limit to their misery."

He sighed a deep sigh and said, "Today it seems there's no limit to your knowledge. It's only today that I've begun to realize that knowledge is the only true source of happiness for man. I'm going to make you my guru. Don't hold anything back."

"I won't hold anything back, which is why you must believe me when I say that there's no happiness to be found in knowledge, nor in truth, in wealth, in the path of devotion, or in family. Man himself weaves these nets of illusory happiness. These birds and beasts and flies and fleas are happier than we. They don't create these mirages of happiness. Whichever form of life they are born into is the one they immerse themselves in. They don't get caught up in all these ridiculous cares and worries as man does. If it were in my hands, I would accept whatever form of life I was given in my next birth – donkey, snake, frog, cow, dog. Any form of life except that of man."

He wanted to say something but he was overcome by a yawn. Then he exclaimed in astonishment, "What kind of crazy talk is that? I don't care what hardships may come, but what can compare to being man? Whether you are a cripple or a leper, a human is a human. A thousand times better than a beast. What! You have no objection to becoming a pig, or a bed bug, a leech, a rat or a flea? Chhi chhi! I am not ready to be anything but human. I don't care if I am offered the chance to be an elephant or a tiger. I give away all this charity just so I'll be born a man in my next birth too. It's fine if I am blind, deaf, a midget, or a mute, but I want a human body. Then I'll sort everything out from there."

"This is the ignorance of man of which he is so proud. At least animals don't entertain such delusions."

He held his head in his hands and said, "I don't need such knowledge then, I don't need it. My ignorance was better."

She tried explaining things to her husband and reached such a pinnacle that it wasn't even in her powers to come down. Strengthening her resolve she said, "Knowledge, ignorance, all this means nothing. These are just labyrinths in the minds of the unenlightened. Only Ram knows when they'll emerge. I don't want to live an illusion in the prison cell of this despicable birth a moment longer. I'm astonished that I have lived all these years in the hope of some kind of happiness! The question keeps playing in my mind: why does man live this insipid, ignorant life? Why?"

Saying this she pulled out a packet of ground diamonds mixed with arsenic and tossed it back before he had even registered what she was doing. The seth couldn't do a thing. His five sons heard his cries and came running, but the sethani had already passed into mukti.

He started crying and wailing with his sons. But would crying bring back the swan of her soul that had departed? Just a few moments ago she had it in her to do all that a human was meant to. To see, talk, listen, smile, sleep, eat, drink, laugh and cry. That same body had suddenly become a lump of clay right before his eyes. In the blink of an eye all activity had ceased and the birdcage was empty. Nature carried on as before.

And who can accompany the dead?

One day she came to the house as a bride. She walked through the door on her own two hennaed feet. And now she was being carried out that same door on others' shoulders. Of what use was all his wealth now? This was the final account of all his charity! He felt as if he were going to suffocate, but even this was an illusion. The husband, the sons and the daughters-in-law all were grieving her loss, but deep inside, their souls were fluttering away and time marched on the same as always. Their eyes watched the funeral pyre burst into a roaring fire. When the ghee and coconut were added to the sandalwood, the flames leapt higher than a bamboo grove. Her golden body turned to ash before their eyes. Left behind were a few bones. The eldest son carried the remains to Haridwar to immerse in the holy Ganga. In all the kingdom there had never been such a third day feast. Then the mourning period ended with the mausar. The Ganga water ceremony was performed. They made offerings to the poor and the brahmins with an open heart. The raja and his courtiers attended the condolence ceremony. Everyone in the kingdom was awed by the seth. But his sad face no longer had its glow. This unforeseen calamity was worse than a nightmare. The sethani was right in saying that nobody could control what happened in this life. The words she spoke before dying burned inside him like a brand on the liver. So he too would have to die someday? And then? After that? Now he had no interest in living, but he knew that in this great cycle of birth and death he couldn't take another birth unless it was a man's. If he had to trade all his wealth and property for this, he wouldn't hesitate. Once you were used to being a man, you couldn't accept anything else. And not just any man, but this very form! It was one in a lakh! Bhagwan himself must envy him. But now he understood very well that he couldn't cause a single leaf in creation to flutter, much less move the moon, the sun, or the wind. When you looked at things this way, all the joy went out of life. There was nothing more wonderful than wealth. Lord Ram knows if it was really such a wonderful thing for man. According to him, the most wonderful thing of all was to take birth in the form of man. Everything else was a waste. Money, knowledge, power, everything. There was nothing holier or greater than being a man. It was only due to man that beauty existed in nature. And it was due to man that Bhagwan came into being. And as for moksha? Well, he didn't have any desire for moksha. He wanted nothing else but to be born a man in his next birth. He had enjoyed his wealth for all it was worth. It was no sin to beg – at least beggars are human after all. The shade of the trees, the veil of the sky, the bed of the earth, and some roots to eat. Bas. He didn't need anything more.

In the end he was no longer able to tamp down all these concerns and so he invited the most well-known pandits in the kingdom to his haveli. He gave each a dakshina of twenty-one coins and asked, "I undertook so many charitable works on the day of the solar eclipse, and these are the fruits? How I have endured the loss of the Sethani only I know. Tell me, is this how the seeds of charity are meant to sprout?"

The pandits immersed themselves in deciphering the Panchanga almanac as if Bhagwan himself had sent envoys. After a while the royal soothsayer came out of his meditation and announced, "Sethji, you should consider it your good fortune that you had only to endure the loss of the Sethani. Otherwise four of your sons too would have joined her in death. It was only through the merit of your charitable works that the inauspicious hour has passed. This is why the Sethani chose to take her own life instead."

The seth turned the soothsayer's words over in his mind trying to make sense of them. Then he asked, "What form of life will this soul of mine take in its next birth?" All the pandits answered as if in one voice, "If you don't wish for moksha, it is up to you. Otherwise you will become whatever form of life you so choose – a mighty emperor, a revered saint, a courageous warrior, or a wealthy seth."

"I have no other desire except that in my next birth I should be a man. With this, all the merit I've accrued in this life shall be rendered worthwhile."

"And is there any doubt, o Annadaata?" said the royal soothsayer.

"Swear on whosoever's head you believe in. Consult the Panchanga and tell me the truth."

The pandits spent quite a while consulting the Panchanga. Either they couldn't understand what was before them, or they could, but were unable or unwilling to tell what they deciphered. But after the seth's persistent prodding, it wasn't possible to stall any longer. The royal soothsayer gathered his courage and announced, "We must respect the honour of your vow, and in any case, I never would tell a lie. If the light from the rising sun is a lie, then so too is what I am about to tell you. I feel ashamed to speak such truth out loud so disgraceful is this munificent soul's next birth."

His heart was trembling. Wiping the perspiration from his face with the end of the gamchha around his neck he said, "Tell me then, what is it? I should know."

The royal soothsayer tried evading, "It would indeed be preferable not to know of one's next birth. Such things are discouraged even in the shastras."

But the seth wouldn't listen no matter what they said. So at last they had to inform him that in his next birth he would be born as a gutter flea in this very haveli.

Hearing this made him nauseous. Fleas started swarming before his eyes. Such a repulsive creature! Is this what he would be in his next birth? His health suffered. It would indeed have been better not to have asked.

His ancestral pandit told him, "Annadaata, how can you have any faith in what they're saying? Invite a reputable pandit from Kashi. Until then you shouldn't worry."

The royal soothsayer rolled up his Panchanga and told him, "The Panchangas are all the same. When read, they will decipher the same truth. It's not in any mortal's power to erase or alter what has been written."

Despite this warning, the seth sent his oldest son off to Kashi by horse.

When he opened his eyes wide, everywhere he looked he saw fleas and more fleas, creeping, crawling, writhing. He rubbed his eyes and still it didn't help. Sleeping-waking, standing-sitting, fleas, fleas and more fleas. As if fleas had taken over all of creation.

All his five sons and their wives were dancing in attendance on him as if on tip-toes. But how could he find any relief? He saw fleas in the food. Fleas in the water. The daughters-in-law would come to fan him and there would be fleas crawling all over their bracelets! He would keep repeating the same words to his sons over and over, "I don't want to become a flea in this lifetime! I feel as if something is taking over my body. Look, are you watching?"

The youngest son sent word to the king and the royal vedic healer flew down by horse the next instant. He gave the seth herbs and roots to keep him from going insane. He came to look in on him throughout the day. The seth would sit up with a start every now and then and start babbling, "These herbs and roots aren't going to do a thing. It's clear: I'm going to turn into a flea in this very life. I don't care how much the cost – if you can find a treatment you know to be completely infallible, just bring it to me."

If it was the kind of concept that could never become clear no matter how full the explanation, how could it possibly become clear to our good seth? All his wealth couldn't help.

The reputable pandit arrived from Kashi. His greed for money made him contradict the royal soothsayer at first, but when the seth made him swear on Ganga Ma, he was forced to tell the truth, "What's the point of worrying uselessly? If worrying ever had any use, you might as well have all the citizens in the land worry about you. Who can control what will happen?"

"Is there no drug even at a seller's price that would make one immortal?"

But no one could do a thing. There was no limit to the agony he suffered at the thought of becoming a flea in his next life.

In truth, there's no bigger healer than time. Gradually the thought of becoming a flea began to fade from his mind. His obsession settled down. He once again started sitting on the front terrace distributing alms by his own hand. He did puja-paath day and night. But eventually he began to withdraw even from these activities and spent his time gazing intently at the many images of creation. He looked at the rising and setting sun as if he were seeing it for the first time, with an interest so keen it seemed he could have swallowed it whole. He looked up at the moon and started dancing, laughing and giggling all the while. He counted each and every star in the sky. He smelled the flowers. Chased after butterflies. Let himself get soaked in the rain. Lost himself in bird songs. Tried mimicking the koyal's sweet calls. He wanted to drink up every last drop of the rasa of human life. Bliss was to be found in creation, not wealth!

Then one day, the same old obsession gripped him anew. As soon as the thought of his next birth entered his head, he felt as if his heart was blazing in a Holi bonfire. One fine moment he was gazing at the rising sun when suddenly he felt a terrible pain in his chest. He shrieked and then started screaming like a madman, "The sun has rotted like a spoiled pumpkin! These fleas have hollowed it out completely! Soon the whole sun is going to break apart and fall!"

The sons came running. The seth was lying on the floor thrashing around, soaked in sweat. They picked him up and laid him on the bed. His eyes were rolling in his head. His body had gone cold. He said in a thick voice, "I'm not a guest in this world much longer. Wash the gutter well with Ganga water. As soon as I stop breathing, look in the gutter. If you see a flea, crush it as soon as you can. I don't want to live the life of a flea for even a moment."

As soon as he said this his teeth clamped together. His eyes turned to stone. His pulse stopped. A moment later his spirit had flown. They laid the corpse on the ground. The middle son ran to look in the gutter. He bent down and peered into it, and there really was a flea creeping about. He picked up a stone and was about to crush it when the joon shouted, "Arey! Are you crazy? I'm perfectly happy here! I'm enjoying myself just fine!"

The son's hand stopped right where it was. He offered, "Just say the word and I will have this gutter covered with a sheet of gold. I'll fill it with Ganga water and flower essence. You must be suffocating in this smelly mud. Chhi! Chhi!"

Gambolling in the mud the flea replied, "Dhatt! How can Ganga water compare to this lovely muck? Even the mention of flower essence makes me want to vomit! What do you know of the joy of this joon? Leave me to look after my own affairs and keep your advice to yourself. Go, do the last rites for your father. Don't worry about me. You can't imagine my happiness. Just look after yourself, that is enough."

the thakur's ghost

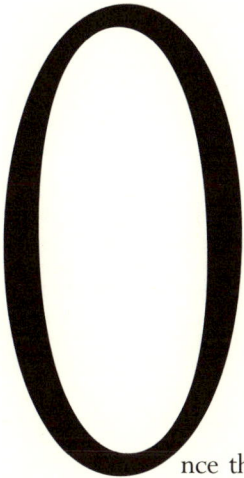

Once there was a thakur of a small basti somewhere whose pretensions were as grand as his estate was modest. His subjects nearly killed themselves working to keep up the standards of a big thikana. Land tariffs and taxes, coercion and cooption so fierce it made you weep. His subjects suffered horribly. And yet they had neither the courage nor the means to leave this place where their ancestors had lived for generations together. The thakur kept up his nasty habits and the people in the basti went on suffering in silence. But no man's status ever helped him defeat mortality, so how could the thakur's? He put up a good fight, but soon his resources were sapped and he headed straight down the road of death at an early age. His body had finished. His spirit was released. But it would not leave the confines of that thikana. The thakur's spirit would circle around from ker bush to khejari tree, from banyan tree to peepal tree, from drinking well to step well. Before too long, people in the area realized that the thakur had become a ghost and was appearing at different places around the outskirts of the thikana.

There was a big farmer in that thikana, the chaudhari of the village who regularly brought in a thousand-maund harvest. But that didn't stop the thakur and his men from giving him trouble. This farmer would labour day and night and still barely got by. Generations had lived life this way and had never had it easy.

Once on Akhateej, the chaudhari lifted his hoe onto his shoulder and headed out to clear his fields, as any good farmer ought to on this holiday. He carried a basket on his head packed with millet roti, saag of green beans, galvani sweets, and cooled water. He had just arrived at the edge of his field when a partridge called – a very inauspicious omen. He paused for a moment, looked around, then went on. This time the partridge didn't call out.

The chaudhari saw a man in sparkling white clothes standing before him under the khejari tree. He walked closer and still he had trouble recognizing who it was. He greeted him and then asked, "Who are you?"

The man in white smiled and said, "Chaudhari! You've garnered so much pride in so little time! I never would have imagined you'd forget the lord of the village so soon! Hardly two moons have gone by since I died."

On hearing this, the chaudhari instantly knew this was the thakur's ghost. But there was no need for fear now. He gathered his courage and said, "Annadaata, this was my first thought. But then I was certain you must already be ruling up in heaven. I thought it was only lowborns like us who turned into ghosts and phantoms and roamed from bush to bush."

Hearing the chaudhari's humble words made the ghost's temper cool. He thought for a moment and said, "Chaudhari, when I was alive I ruled for all I was worth. But now I have no desire to rule. If I tell you the truth you will not believe it: I have chosen not to establish my raj up in heaven just so that I can stay here on earth and look after you farmers. When I was alive I made my subjects suffer terribly. Now that I am a ghost, I will watch over your fields. I want to make good all my wrongs and compensate you somehow."

The chaudhari clicked his tongue and said, "Annadaata, why tip a boulder to crush a few ants? We've taken birth only to serve you, my lord. We are your hands and feet, working for you day and night. I wouldn't call it suffering."

The thakur began sweetly, "Truly Chaudhari, when I was alive my arrogance was one thing, but now that I'm dead, I see things differently. I worked you to death during my short lifetime. And when I died I couldn't take even a fistful of grain with me. I had to leave the four walls of my thikana empty-handed. Now the pandits are there every day doing their puja-paath, so I can't go near the place. Why would the prince and the thakurani have anything to do with me now? People weep and mourn and carry on only when it's in their own interest. I ached to go back to my domain, but they didn't let me set foot inside. So now I'm regretting with all my heart that I made you suffer so much just for them. I want to ease your burden somehow so I can find peace of mind."

The chaudhari started weeping in his heart. He had never heard such sweet words from his lord's mouth before. He clasped his hands and said: "My burden has been lifted just receiving such grace from your noble mouth."

The thakur's ghost interrupted, "Burdens aren't lifted just with words. I really want to do something for you people. Tell me Chaudhari, how many maunds of grain do you harvest every year?"

The chaudhari said, "Annadaata, this isn't something that's hidden from you. In a good year it has never been below a thousand maunds."

The ghost said, "And of that you wouldn't even get to keep a hundred. Today my soul writhes in agony to think of the crimes I committed against you people. Listen to me, there's no need for you to plough a single furrow from now on. You go back home the way you came. I'll see to it that you get two thousand maunds of millet this autumn harvest. And you're not to give a single grain to the thikana. They don't deserve it!"

The chaudhari shook his head, "No Annadaata, Lord Ram protect us from such ill-gotten gains. Beasts of burden like us can't compare to big people like you. Hearing such nectar-filled words from your noble mouth it's as if I've been blessed with not just a thousand maunds but a harvest a lakh strong instead. But Annadaata, lowly folk like us, after these many generations, have got used to eating the fruits of our own labour, so are unable to digest anything else. We'd rather die than sit around not doing any work."

The thakur's ghost didn't at all like what the chaudhari said. But he held his anger in check and said, "Do you mean to say that all of us thakurs only eat the fruits of others' labour? That we gulp down ill-gotten gains?"

The chaudhari clasped his hands right up to his elbows and folded in on himself, pleading, "Annadaata, how could such a statement ever have slipped from these lips? This mouth is not on loan from somewhere that I'd use it to defame my lord! The work you big people have to do is taking it easy, as a result of the karma in your past birth. According to our karma, we have to labour and toil. That such grace has come from your royal mouth is more than enough."

The ghost stepped up close and said through gnashed teeth, "Nothing happens through mere words, it's all in the doing. There's no need for you to set a single foot in these fields after this. You don't have to do anything but sit there, and two thousand maunds of millet will appear. Then you will be able to judge for yourself how true my words are. It will be good for you peasant types to suffer a little by taking it easy for once. After all, we've had to endure such suffering for generations."

The chaudhari was stuck. He didn't want to take the millet without earning it, and he also didn't want to argue with the ghost. After all, this wasn't just any ghost but the thakur's. Displease him and he could destroy his home. He thought a little and then said, "Annadaata, if you'll allow me, I'd like to sow a good auspice on this day of Akhateej."

The ghost bellowed, "I've appeared to you after death — what better auspice do you need than *that*?! Rest assured you will get your two thousand maunds of millet. Now go home and tap the drums of rest and leisure. There's no need for you to even head in the direction of these fields."

The thakur's ghost wouldn't listen no matter what he said, so the chaudhari had to walk back home without having luffed up a single chigdo of dirt with his hoe. He had heard plenty of stories about the marvellous feats of ghost and phantoms. Nothing was beyond their powers. If the ghost had promised to produce two thousand maunds of millet, then surely he'd be good as his word. But despite this, the chaudhari wasn't too happy. How could he agree to reap a harvest that he hadn't himself sown?

When he got home he couldn't keep what happened from the chaudharan and told her the whole story. When she heard, the chaudharan became livid as a cobra whose tail has been stepped on. She said, "If we haven't earned it ourselves, we don't need a single speck of that ill-gotten grain. Such indolence won't be erased for seven generations. Much better we die of hunger!"

Then all of a sudden the chaudharan started laughing. "I never knew you were so simple-hearted!" she chuckled. "There was no limit to the misery the thakur put us through when he was alive. And now that he's dead, do you really believe his ghost is going to start bestowing boons on us?! Well, you can believe him all you want, but I wouldn't trust him even in my wildest dreams."

The chaudhari said, "A man can be as brave as one would wish, but stand him in front of a ghost and he can't help but turn simple-hearted. I too had great difficulty swallowing the idea, but how could I have put my foot down? I didn't want him to get annoyed and start troubling our boys. So I bowed to his will."

The chaudharan began to worry at the mention of their sons. She controlled her rage and said, "I don't believe a shred of what he says. But if he truly does make good on his promise, I don't think we should allow a single grain of that harvest into our house. We'll send half to the thikana and feed the other half to the pigeons. And we'll carry on as if there's been a drought. Pretend as if Indra the Lord of Rain has unleashed his dry, scalding fury on us."

Husband and wife thus reassured themselves somehow or the other. But as soon as the monsoon month of Asarh arrived, Bhagwan Indra found it in his good grace to send down unending drainpipes of rain. As if the clouds themselves had forgotten how to stop. There was water and still more water everywhere you looked.

After so many days the soil had reached the crumbly vatai stage, which everyone knows is perfect for ploughing. All the farmers in the village were beside themselves with joy as they hitched up their ploughs and urged their teams of bullocks on towards the fields. The village chaudhari couldn't restrain himself any longer. He harnessed his Nagauri bullocks and set out for his fields. As he was leaving, he called out to his fieldhands to ready eight teams of ploughs and head to the fields as soon as he sent word.

The thakur's ghost was standing under the same khejari tree. As soon as the chaudhari greeted him he asked, "I told you over and over, so why are you coming here with your bullocks all harnessed? You don't trust my word?"

The chaudhari reined in his bullocks and said, "No Baapji, I don't have it in me to distrust anything you've said. But I've never seen such rains for as long as I can remember. And so I thought, whatever we gather with our two hands to eat, it's the same as if it had been given to us by your own hand. May I submit this one truth, that until today I have never before sat idle. As soon as the rains come, my veins begin to swell they want so badly to get to work. I came to the field just to draw a few token furrows, Annadaata."

The ghost shook his head and said, "Oh-ho, this year I will not let you set foot on these fields. You people used to curse us landlords and nobles for living the life of luxury, hands folded behind our heads. Now you see how hard it is to sit around doing nothing but enjoying yourselves. It's only been a little while, and you've had enough already? You have to give us credit, we feudal types wouldn't even chase the flies sitting on our faces ourselves if we could help it. It's always been like this, in this world a man always feels his own unhappiness and others' happiness more. You've got to admire our fortitude that we endured this life of luxury without a word of complaint. Didn't let out even a sigh of protest."

The chaudhari couldn't do anything with this ghost staring him down except swallow the rancid dal and go back the way he'd come. The ghost wouldn't let him pull a single weed or plough a single furrow. All the other fields in the area had been ploughed and looked as soft and light and pretty as sweet magad, while the chaudhari's field was packed down solid, hard and ugly, like talra ground dried after floods. He didn't say anything to anyone. He wandered about forlornly gazing at others' fields. Here and there people would ask him why hadn't he worked his fields, but he'd just become vague and evade their questions. When he saw the green shoots of millet unfurling, the image of his gray, colourless fields pricked him like a splinter in the eye. Now what was he to do? He wandered about aimlessly and finally arrived back at his fields. That donkey of a ghost hadn't left his place under the khejari. As soon as the chaudhari's eyes fell on him he started pleading, "O Annadaata, green shoots of millet have begun unfurling in all the fields except in my colourless ones. How are we to reap a harvest that hasn't even begun to sprout yet?"

The thakur cut him off with a sharp laugh, "Reaping grain, that's the human way of working. All we godly types have to do is make a wish and take in a lakh maund of grain. Are you only going to turn this over to me when a sudden drought or an early flood wipes out your crops? I told you so many times and still you haven't given up your old ways?"

The chaudhari contained his temper and said, "If we have laboured and toiled in our fields and still don't get a single grain, at least we have some consolation for ourselves. But if we don't do any work at all and leave our fields fallow, we might as well shoot ourselves in the gut. Annadaata, it's not too late, allow me to start ploughing my fields. I feel as if I'm going mad sitting around doing nothing."

The ghost laughed a belly-rolling laugh and said, "Now you understand, don't you, that in this world there's nothing more difficult than taking it easy. And here you people used to see us and feel jealous. Chaudhari, there's no greater happiness than that gained from labour."

The chaudhari and the ghost argued plenty, but the ghost wouldn't listen and he wouldn't agree. And he wouldn't let that chaudhari plough a single furrow.

In the other millet fields they had already weeded and straightened the rows, tidied up the furrows. Plant upon plant grew from each root, clustered together thick and strong. The heads of millet were so laden they hung to the ground. And still more shoots sprouted from the nodes on their stems. The millet fields swayed in the breeze as if they would lift the ground right off the earth. The chaudhari looked at his gray, colourless fields and felt his liver sear. He went before the ghost again and again with folded hands, begging and pleading. But the ghost wouldn't even let him utter the word ploughing. The chaudhari started beseeching him in earnest, so the thakur replied through gnashed teeth, "This is a test I'm giving you people. These ill-gotten gains haven't even touched your palms and already you're wasting your breath crying hai-hai. This is no easy job. It's only stout-hearted people like us who could live on others' labour for generation after generation without uttering so much as a sigh."

The chaudhari said, "I pinch my ears in remorse a thousand times, Annadaata, a thousand times. To tell the truth, it'd be better to go up in flames than to sit around idle. We are indeed better off than you feudals. It is a great boon that you highborns have hearts stout enough to endure such suffering."

The ghost said, "You people have been making us suffer the ignominy of living off other people's labour for generations. Who knows how much misery you have caused us, so grant us this one opportunity to make you suffer in turn. It's only been this one time, and you are raising such a fuss. I tell you over and over, and still I find you running all over the place."

The chaudhari was trapped whichever way he turned. If he went to the fields the ghost wouldn't let him pass, and if he went home he wouldn't get any peace. He was alive and healthy and well, and still his fields were completely fallow. The heads of millet in all the other fields were as round and strong as a hand-forged argata. The millet had grown so tall that a man riding a camel would disappear behind it, while his field was bare as a bald head. The villagers started making fun of the chaudhari. He didn't feel at peace unless he was walking in his fields. Each time he'd arrive there the ghost would be ready and waiting. The chaudhari surrendered his turban at the ghost's feet and said, "Annadaata, if I had been working these fields, I'd get a yield of two and a half thousand maunds of millet. There hasn't been a harvest like this in fifty years. The millet has grown so high it might have cracked hell apart. It's grown so thick in their fields you couldn't throw a spear through it if you tried. I don't know what kind of crops could ever come from these parched fields of mine. You could make a wish right now and have it appear just like that. I beg you to bestow your grace upon my fields and grow the finest millet crop of all. Let me do the threshing at least. Let me do *some*thing. I can't sleep, I can't eat."

The ghost said, "No. This time your storage bhakhariyas will be filled without you. You just wait and watch what kind of miracles I'm capable of."

The chaudhari set his turban at the ghost's feet again and said, "Baapji, if you want to show your miracles then show them in the fields. Even after cutting the grain, we still have plenty of work to do before we finish threshing: chopping it, stacking it into bundles and then into bales, propping the bundles into stacks to dry and separating the head from the straw to spread out on the threshing floor. May I please satisfy my habit of indulging in labour? If I enjoy the fruits without the sweat, then it works on me like poison. I'd gladly take one thousand maunds instead of two, but when I don't do any work it feels like someone's set a boulder on my chest."

The ghost remained as rigidly stubborn as ever and the chaudhari was left with nothing but his burning desire to work. The ghost said, "If it'd make you happy I'll grant you four thousand maunds instead of two, but I won't let you even utter the word work. Pretend as if you're sick in bed for the four months of the monsoon."

The chaudhari scratched his head and replied, "I'm perfectly fit and healthy. How am I going to pretend to myself that I'm sick?"

The chaudhari returned home upset and dejected. He couldn't get in the mood to do anything. The chaudharan started teasing him to get his mind off his troubles, "Is the Thakur's ghost going to take someone else's millet from the threshing floor to fulfill his promise? If he really wants to show off his miraculous powers, why take so long? He doesn't have to raise the crops himself, you know!"

Seeing his mind was still on his troubles she pushed a little harder, "Why are you getting all upset needlessly? If you'd rather, I won't put a single grain of that millet in our handi to cook. I'll throw it to the pigeons, I won't do anything you don't want."

It felt like a spear piercing his liver whenever he thought of the blessings Bhagwan Indra had rained down on the village, while his field remained flat as a racecourse at Gangaur. His fields, too, could have been stacked tight with mounds of straw, with millet growing so thick it would trap even a deer's nimble leg.

The chaudharan said only the kindest, most cheerful words to her husband, but there was no getting his mind off his troubles. The next day he again walked towards his fields like a man crazed. Thakur-sa's ghost walked up to him smiling and asked, "Chaudhari, you certainly have a long face today. What happened?"

The chaudhari said, "Baapji, you dwell in each and every heart. How can I hide from you what's burning inside me? I implore you with hands clasped not to deliver the millet to our storage bhakhariyas but instead to pile the heads of millet in the fields. Then I can do all the work by my own hand — pounding it, sifting out the grain from the chaff, then marking it with a protective doon-deni design. My bones ache when I don't work."

The ghost said, "Chaudhari, just imagine what state my bones must have been in sleeping on that thick mattress all those years. And I never once wrinkled my nose. You've barely had a little rest, and you're already this bothered?"

The chaudhari said, "Annadaata, you big people are in another category altogether, while I'm the sort who would want to work even after I'm dead. If only you'll allow me in your infinite grace to do some kind of work, I'll sing your praises, offer incense and oblations to your image as long as I live."

The thakur's ghost said, "I've already said No once; I'm not going to use this same mouth to say Yes. If you hadn't been harrowed like this, how would you have ever known the suffering we highborns have endured? Don't give it a second or third thought, I'm going to bestow upon you millet as hard and shiny white as a parad snake's pearly eye."

What more could the chaudhari say? He set off silently for home. The chaudharan talked nonstop trying to cheer him up, but it was useless. He sat glooming around the hut for three days. On the fourth day he went to that khejari tree again. The noonday sun was high overhead. The thakur hadn't budged from his spot.

The chaudhari greeted him and immediately announced, "Annadaata, if you don't honour my request today, I am ready to commit suicide. Everyone else is exhausting themselves out hauling away cartloads of millet. What a year it's been, as if it were raining down sweet pearls of millet. Please, if you would just clap your hands right here and now and make the piles of millet appear. Then at least I'll get to cart it away."

The thakur's ghost heard the chaudhari and began hooting with laughter and wouldn't stop for quite some time. Still chuckling he said, "Chaudhari, I've seen many lunatics in this world, but none to match you. You really believed that I was going to make good on my promise and see that you received all that millet? You poor kala, I devoted so much of my time alive ensuring that you suffered; if I were to now start trying to make you happy, I'd wind up going straight to hell! You would never have listened to me if I hadn't given you that promise. The harvest would have been the best in the region, and I would never have been able to stomach that! You two will just have to enjoy that millet in your dreams."

But the chaudhari was immensely relieved to hear the thakur's ghost. "You have bestowed the greatest boon of all upon us, o Annadaata, in lifting this burden off our backs. It doesn't bother me one bit that you didn't bestow grain into our waiting hands. If you had filled our idle hands with grain, I would have been miserable. There is a deep bond between the earth and our sweat. We'll be raising millet for as long as we stand. I'm going to distribute twenty five ser of gur in my infinite gratitude for being saved the ignominy of receiving ill-gotten grain!"

Then the chaudhari said farewell and set off for home feeling light as a flower. How happy the chaudharan was to see his glowing face! She asked, "Did you witness the Thakur's miracle? Not a single grain of millet has come to our home yet."

When the chaudhari spoke, the words rained down like sweet pearls, "It's a good thing such ill-gotten grain has not entered this house, nor will it. The Thakur has died but he hasn't changed." And the chaudhari began to narrate the whole tale for her patiently. The chaudharan was overjoyed. She said, "When he was still alive, he used the pretext of lagaan to take more than his fair share. And now that he's dead, he's not letting us grow grain in our own fields. What else can we expect from big people like him? It's only by Bhagwan's good grace that ill-gotten grain didn't go down our children's throats."

For the first time in days the chaudhari slipped into a deep, carefree sleep. He had the loveliest, sweetest dreams. In his dreams he worked and he laboured, he laboured and he toiled. And all that toil brought a sheen of sweat to his skin. And from that sweat they were able to reap countless, priceless pearls.

alexander and the crow

Hail Alexander the Great! But when Alexander the Great comes down with a fever like any other man, where is all his greatness then? He didn't have the energy even to mull further on this question hissing in his ear, so he simply rang the bell. Just at that moment an Ionian soldier presented himself in full armour and helmet. In his right hand he held a double-bladed sword, in his left hand a long spear. He bowed three times and awaited orders. Alexander meant to convey something in his glare, but couldn't speak for all the coughing. The tall, robust soldier came forward like a puppet on a string. He bowed with an adaab, then lifted up the silver spittoon and stood by the bed. The emperor coughed three or four times, spit a gob of phlegm into the spittoon and then collapsed back onto the bed, exhausted. Alexander's throat was full of gummy, dirty snot just like any ordinary soldier's. The soldier wiped off the phlegm stuck on his lord's lips and poured water from a silver amphora so he could rinse out his mouth. Alexander cast his eyes up to the ceiling with a cold glance and issued a command, "Three days have passed and not a single one of the Ionian treatments has worked. We shall have the hakim's head soon enough, but first I want you to sift through every corner of the Punjab and find an experienced vaid. The fever has hardly abated, and the head and body aches have only increased. I cannot sleep. All those medicines have only made my health worse. Be quick! If a vaid does not appear by evening, I will slaughter everyone in the camp. Here I am dying of fever, and you people are roaming around healthy as can be. Have you no shame? You are all disgraceful, absolutely disgraceful! If I learn that any soldier has eaten before my fever has come down, then it's his neck. Now go! Why are you standing there staring at me like that?"

Barely a half hour had passed before the soldier was back. Alexander opened his eyes and asked, "You informed everyone?"

"It was not necessary, Cherisher of the Poor," the soldier said, half bowing, "Hindustan's most respected vaid has come here of his own accord."

Alexander made an effort to smile, but couldn't. He lashed out in dismay, "This is indeed a strange land! I have conquered so many lands but never seen a place like this! But where is he? Why did you not bring him with you?"

"He is standing outside waiting, Huzur! If it is your command, I shall bring him in at once."

"Stop this nonsense!" He snapped angrily, "Have I to issue an order for such a thing? You only make use of that brain in your head when it is the appointed time for it to work, is it? Hurry up and bring him to me now!"

He had shouted so loudly that the vaid standing outside came in without being asked. He smiled and said, "There's no need to call me. I made use of the brain in my head and came myself."

Alexander was startled to see a man with a long, sparkling white beard. Long, white hair. A broad, impressive brow. Shining white teeth. A sharp nose. Eyes that spilled over with love and kindness. As if some divine emissary had appeared before him. The emperor forgot his illness for a moment.

The vaid gazed thoughtfully at the face and eyes of the sick man lying in bed, his face glowing like an Ionian god. A touch of languor from this recent illness. Eyes frenzied in arrogance. Thick, black eyebrows. Thin, pink lips. Long, strong arms. A body so strong and fit it seemed to have been cast in a mold.

A vision of his esteemed guru Aristotle's tender gaze flashed before Alexander's eyes. He was about to say something but the next instant he began coughing so hard his ears buzzed. He stuck out his arm so the physician could take his pulse. The elderly vaid shook his head and said, "No, we begin our preliminary diagnosis by looking at a patient's face and eyes rather than taking his pulse. This looks like a periodic fever — internal pyrexia. It's not going to let up in less than seventeen days." He paused for a moment and then continued, "There's no use going over what you have been eating and drinking uptil now. But from today onwards you are to stop ingesting meat, wine and anything else that's hard on the system. Even after the fever lifts, you will have to follow my orders very strictly. Otherwise there's a danger the fever could return in a more virulent form."

The conquerer of the world trembled within. This warrior who had taken thousands of lives was terrified at the prospect of his own death. Stammering slightly he asked, "Danger? What danger? How could an ordinary fever be dangerous? What do you mean by this? Tell me straight."

"This is no ordinary fever. You have spent three days enjoying those things which should have been forbidden, and this has made your situation much worse. Treat it now with all the precautions, and we shall have it under control. Otherwise not."

Both the emperor and his soldier could not bear to hear what the vaid was telling them. The soldier clasped the hilt of his sword. Alexander was furious, "Do you know what happens to people who refuse to obey the emperor? And I am Alexander. *Alexander!* Have you never heard of my glory?"

"I've heard quite a bit. I've even seen it with my own eyes," said the vaid, and then added without artifice, "How could anyone forget the massacre of the Punjab?"

The emperor seemed immersed in thought. The vaid understood just by looking at him. He was about to say something more when Alexander sighed deeply and said, "And yet you came of your own will to treat me. This I do not understand."

The old man smiled. He came closer, looked straight into Alexander's eyes and said, "There is no great mystery in this. I maintain complete loyalty towards my country, and at the same time I fulfill my duty towards the sick. These are two separate things. Mixing the two up would only lead to trouble."

"The sick? You said the sick? I am Alexander! Alexander the Great! The first Conquerer of the World! Do you have any sense at all?"

"I am fully in my senses. Otherwise how could I have come without being called? I need no other sense than this. But please, I beg of you let us leave aside this matter. I have brought everything you will need for your treatment, except for one root I will need to find in the forest." And the vaid left the room without waiting for permission.

Alexander ordered his men, "I want two soldiers with him every moment."

"At your command, Protector of the World!"

And the Protector of the World said quietly to himself, "Such strange people! Every child, every old man, every woman – each one a philosopher. How can my guru Aristotle consider every non-Ionian a slave to be auctioned off? How is this right? I shall make a treaty with Porus and decide to settle here."

As skilled and wise a healer that the elderly vaid was, he had little understanding of the complexities of politics. So having made the decoction, he came right back from the forest. He insisted that Alexander drink from an oyster shell brimming over, "I will care for you myself and feed you this potion every three hours."

The soldier leapt forward, grabbed the oyster shell before the emperor even had a chance to refuse and declared, "You will have to take a sip of this yourself first. This is the law."

Alexander wanted to hide his weakened condition, and so he sat up straight. He gazed at the old vaid's beard as innocently as a child and said, "In case there might be a life-threatening poison mixed in." And the next moment an otherworldly smile glimmered on his lips. "But I am ready to drink even poison if it be served by your hand. Ma Olympias used to give me medicine just like this when I was a child, in an oyster shell exactly like this." Then he opened his mouth and the vaid fed him the decoction from the oyster shell. How astonishing that the mighty Ionian emperor had become a child once again. He snatched away the oyster shell and began licking it clean unselfconsciously.

Then his eyes clouded over as he placed the dirty shell in the hands of the soldier. His heart was overflowing with a profound joy. He couldn't lie back down even though he wanted to. He sat up a little longer. Then he asked the vaid, "How did you know about my illness? You never asked anyone nor did anyone inform you."

"The same way that birds know where to find water. The way bumblebees find flowers and honeybees pollen." Then allowing himself a faint smile, the elderly vaid added, "The way vultures and crows find a dying animal."

Alexander did not see room for a reply, and so he just sat gazing at the silver-coloured beard.

Early the next morning as he was giving Alexander his dose, the vaid warned him, "For about five to eight hours you will feel a burning in your chest, pain throughout your body, a headache, and restlessness. Do not worry. Just take courage and carry on. In the meantime, only drink water that has been boiled with the sparkling sand of the river bank, and eat only half-roasted millet mash and goat's milk. After three days, it will be beneficial to ingest figs boiled in cow's milk. I fully trust that you'll be healthier than you were before."

It all happened just as the vaid had predicted. The emperor's health gradually deteriorated and kept getting worse for five to eight hours. The conqueror of the world was in desperate straits. He had thousands of soldiers in his army. So strong and true, they'd offer up their blood as if it were sweat. Their loyalty was absolute. But no one could share his sickness with him. He had to endure it whichever way he could. Alone. It felt as if a glowing ember had been set inside his chest. His palms burned. The soles of his feet burned. His viscera crept and writhed. The emperor of the world tossed and turned like a child. He lay there in a half-conscious state encountering experiences so incredible, so strange they were beyond speech or language. He forgot all about the prestige and glory of the Ionians and the Macedonians. The man whose victory bugles blew all over Persia, Egypt, Syria, Africa and Central Asia was now lying all by himself sick in bed. Silent. Even his wife Roxanna could not share his suffering. When the citizens of Thebes had railed against their servitude, he rumbled through like an earthquake destroying everything in the city. Six thousand inhabitants who moments before had been living and breathing, laughing, smiling, dreaming – he hacked them to death. Now they were dreamless. He captured thousands of women and children and sold them into slavery. Now they were all coming before him demanding an account for each breath he had stolen. The founder of seventy new cities lay there helpless in a tiny room. His condition could not be remedied by all the diamonds and pearls in the world, nor by countless gold and silver. He could only watch as light and dark flashed before his eyes.

But as soon as the five to eight hours had passed, he opened his eyes – it was as if the curse of a nightmare were suddenly over. The first thing he was aware of was having barely escaped death. It was useless to put any faith in those Ionian healers. The emperor looked at the vaid with eyes of gratitude, and the vaid looked back at his patient as affectionately as a parent gazing at his child. So much was expressed in that moment of silence that couldn't possibly have been said by a saliva-coated tongue.

It was only by suffering through such a terrible illness that the conqueror began to understand the value of life – just as the sun rises only once a day, so man is given only one life to live. No one lives twice. But Alexander had never stopped to consider this simple truth before. In battle after battle, massacre after massacre, he had never had time to realize that he too was mortal. Even after he had joined the divine, the world would go on just as it had before — that this was the only truth. And he had never been so indifferent to worldly ambition as he was at this moment. After much thought and cogitation, he scratched his neck and asked the vaid doubtfully, "If you had not come to treat me, tell me, would I have died?"

The vaid was waiting just for this moment. "No. You still have many years to live," he replied.

"How many? How many years do I have left?" Alexander asked.

"Why do you want to know? It is better not to know. This is as true for the king as for the beggar."

"I cannot bear the thought that all the countless citizens of this world will go on living even after I am gone. That the sun and moon will keep on rising even without me, that flowers will still blossom, people will celebrate their nuptials, and sing festive songs to new mothers, and bathe in the rain — No! I am absolutely unable to suffer the thought. It just cannot be possible that Alexander would depart from this world while some insignificant, common man will go on living and breathing and laughing and smiling."

"And yet it happens just like that," the vaid said in a quiet firm voice. "Your esteemed father passed away and yet the world lives on. It happens just like that, and it always will."

"No, he didn't just pass away, he was killed."

"Death doesn't take responsibility for her deeds. All she needs is the slightest excuse. And when it comes, bas, that's enough for her."

"But in my case I'm not going to give her the slightest excuse."

"Such excuses come of their own accord, Death doesn't have to go looking for them." Then he added, "Do you really wish to be immortal? I wouldn't."

Alexander didn't pause a moment before replying, "What temptations do you have in your life that would make you wish to be immortal? My life is full of such temptations – so many victorious empires, thousands of slaves, unimaginable wealth, countless diamonds and pearls and endless stores of gold and silver. The world has never before seen the likes of an emperor such as me – one who possesses such a vast empire and so much wealth! Have I shed so much blood just in order to die at a chance moment?"

The vaid thought the matter over a little and replied, "If you have such a burning desire to become immortal, then I will tell you a way. No one but I knows of it. But you need to promise me that you will not share this secret with anyone."

Alexander's joy knew no bounds; it was as if all the stars and the sky had suddenly come into his fist. If he'd had ten or twenty more tongues in his head, they would have all shouted out in unison. He was emperor of the world, but still had only one tongue, "No, I absolutely promise I will not tell a soul. Not even Roxanna, the person I'm closest to in this life. Anyway, why should women become immortal? They might as well die after they turn twenty. Oh, and I don't want to grow old as time passes, I want to stay exactly as I am now."

The old vaid sat there a while striking a philosophical pose. Then he said in a voice so patient and full it was as if his words were like rain in the still air of Alexander's room, "I pray that Parameshwar the Supreme Lord grant you good judgement. Do I have to remind you that when you were first born, you were just as helpless, submissive and powerless as any other? It was only in time that you grew bigger, became an adolescent. And so too in time you will become a weak, cowardly, decrepit old man just like any other transitory being. Even if we leave aside the matter of an untimely death, you must realize that we value life only due to this everlasting blessing called death. You took Lord Yamraj's work into your own two hands and saw to it that thousands of innocents met untimely ends. And *you* want to be immortal? Why?"

This was the first time in his life that someone had opposed his wishes, and yet Alexander did not lose his temper. Because he longed for immortality, and this old man was the only one who knew how to obtain it. Besides, this vaid had saved his life. He felt he hadn't fully explained his side of things, and so started talking off the top of his head, "Only because never before has there been such a vast empire, never before has anyone possessed so much wealth. And so I cannot rid myself of this desire. Immortality is what I want more than anything else — what I want and what I need."

This time, not only the old vaid's teeth and lips but every hair of his beard seemed to sparkle with an otherworldly smile. Nodding his head to signal his acceptance he said, "I will not say anything more. I am not sure why I had hoped a student of a guru as great as Aristotle would have a different understanding. Well, I would certainly not wish to leave your final yearning unfulfilled. We will not meet again after this. But my blessings shall always be with you. As soon as I return to my ashram I will deliver one last exposition to my disciples and then leave this world by entering eternal samadhi. So you must listen carefully. On the west side of Mount Sumeru is a deep cave. At its mouth is a huge boulder. Have your most trusted soldiers move the boulder aside and wait while you venture inside alone, unafraid and unarmed. Yours will be the first footprints to leave their mark on that unblemished ground."

The vaid was quiet for some time, observing what lay beneath Alexander's strong body, watching the emotions churn within him. Then he continued, "After walking a ways you will see clearly before you a pond where water from a waterfall has collected. This pond never empties nor does it ever overflow. There a crow sits on the branch of a peepal tree calling, Kraw! Kraw! Kraw! This is the only eternal being in all creation, he who shrieks for his immortality every waking moment. Draw seven handfuls of water from the current of this never-ceasing waterfall. Then none will be able to threaten your life – neither god, nor demon, nor man. Take with you only twenty one of your most trusted soldiers. Keep them posted three thousand paces from the mouth of the cave. You must depart on the ninth day of the waxing fortnight. Then your heart's desire will be fulfilled."

After that how could Alexander delay? As if in a golden dream, he and his twenty one well-armed soldiers flew as fast as the wind to Mount Sumeru and arrived at the mouth of the cave. Even with the combined strength of those soldiers, they could barely push that boulder far enough to allow him to slip in. He entered the darkness of the cave and was struck by a thought. If any of Porus's men were waiting inside to attack him, then how could he fend off an attack defenseless and alone? He had never before experienced such an overpowering fear of death. Rather than giving in to his strong desire to run back like a coward, he immediately stepped forward to face his fear head on. No, no, that guileless divine emissary of India would not betray even his enemy. He remembered how the vaid's snowy beard had sparkled in reassurance, then he continued forward, unafraid. And truly, there sat a crow on the branch of a big, broad peepal tree, repeating the same chant of immortality over and over, Kraw! Kraw! Kraw! Nearby, the waterfall never ceased flowing, its honeyed gurgling echoing throughout the cave. On finding a faint light so deep inside the cave, Alexander's wonder knew no bounds. He looked again with eyes wide open and realized with a start that there were priceless diamonds scattered everywhere! The rays from this incomparable radiance were altogether distinct from the light of the sun or the full moon. He saw no other being there besides the crow. Was the crow the guardian of all these unimaginable riches? Did he even realize how much treasure he was in possession of? He would drink the water and then think of a plan for seizing all these gems. Nothing was impossible for Alexander!

Suddenly, the crow's neverending kraw-kraw-kraw ceased. Alexander looked at the peepal tree, startled. The crow was staring at him unflinchingly. Surely he couldn't have discerned his most secret desire! The uninterrupted flow of the waterfall abruptly ceased, as if someone had clenched it in invisible, bloodthirsty claws. The unbearable stillness of that silence pierced his ears. Then the light snuffed out completely and he could neither see his way to the waterfall nor leave the cave. In such eternal and endless darkness he would be trapped in that cave until he would surely petrify. Then a hazy mist spread out before Alexander and something beyond his control led his feet towards the waterfall, as if his feet were doing the thinking.

He was so mesmerized by the desire for immortality that his hands began to reach out blindly in the direction of the water when he heard the crow call out – "Alexander wait!" He stopped right where he was. The crow continued, "If you drink a single drop of that water without my permission, you'll be reduced to a heap of rubble. You would not want to make the same mistake I once made even in a dream, a mistake that has forced me to suffer these thousands upon thousands of years living out the curse of immortality. I have sickened of this eternal life. I know not how many centuries it has been that I have wanted to die, but I cannot. Repeating kraw-kraw over and over my ears have turned deaf. Indeed, I am the undisputed lord of all this wealth that has awakened your desire. If you go to Yamraj and secure from him a way by which I can end my life, I will gladly surrender all these riches to you. Now it pains my eyes even to behold it. Once I am dead, you can drink all the water you want from this pond. But unfortunately, I cannot die by that hand of yours that has felled so many brave soldiers. I cannot burn in fire, I cannot drown in water, I cannot kill myself by taking even the most potent of poisons. Even if Bhagwan himself were to cease to be, still I would not die. The joy of life, its happiness exists only when bound to the certainty of death. There is no curse worse than that of death-deprived immortality. It is my everlasting ill-fortune that I must endure this tragedy. Arey! What thought are you immersed in now? If you were to place a value on the living breath of any one man you have felled in battle, of any child you have sold into slavery, all this impossible wealth you see before you would not be worth a single cowrie shell. If I can understand such a simple thing in this manifestation as a crow, how can you as a man fail to comprehend it? What then is the meaning of intelligence? How can it be considered meaningful? Kraw! Kraw! Kraw!"

Even in this moment of his greatest ascendency, despite all his supreme renown, Alexander the conqueror of the world was forced to concede to a crow and follow his footprints back the way he had come.

So of the two, who do you think is greater – Alexander or the crow?

to each her own

Fish survive on water and fishermen on fish. It just so happened that once upon a time and place there was a fresh water lake. And at the edge of this lake was a fisherman's hut. In front of the hut was a freshly mud-plastered aangan in which all kinds of fish were laid out to dry in the sun. There were fish on the roof of the hut, fish hanging from hooks on the rafters inside, fish tucked into every crook and corner of the small hut. The air was thick with the odour of fish. But the hut's inhabitants were accustomed to it.

Everyday, the fisherwoman would fill her basket with fish and walk to the nearest town to sell them. One overcast monsoon day, as she was heaving the basket onto her head all set to leave, her husband cautioned her, "The sky looks ominous. Hurry back. I'm worried the river will flood." Then he smiled and continued, "If the river is flowing full, do not set foot near it. That would ruin my life. I can hardly go and set up house a third time."

The fisherwoman turned and smiled, "Don't worry, I value my life too."

They say once someone scalds his tongue on hot milk, thereafter he'll always blow on even buttermilk before sipping it – the fisherman had that kind of caution. His previous wife had drowned just the year before in that very river. She had waded into the water thinking it was knee-deep, only to have the roaring rapids knock her off her feet. She thrashed and kicked to stay afloat, but it was no use.

Fishermen have a keen sense of the signs of damp, wind, and rain. The fisherwoman had barely crossed the riverbed and entered town when it started pouring. Within minutes she was drenched right through. She began to panic and hurriedly sold off all her fish for whatever little they fetched. And then she ran back as fast as she could. But by the time she reached the water's edge, the river had already swelled to fearsome proportions, such enormous waves their very sight scared her. Rapids steep as mountains tumbled down roiling up whatever came in their path.

She remembered her husband's warning and turned around at once. But where would she go? Some stranger's basti? Where would she spend the night? Fortunately, just then she saw the gardener coming down the road towards her. The raja's beautiful gardens were nearby. She had finished her housework and was now coming to keep watch over the garden. The two had met several times before on this road, and usually just said their salaams and greetings to each other and walked on. Work to do. A living to make.

As soon as the gardener saw the fisherwoman's face, she understood why she was upset and said, "The river has come up, but so what? Come with me. There'll be plenty of room." The fisherwoman's heart filled with gratitude as she turned to follow the gardener.

The rain was easing up. They had walked some distance when the gardener noticed that the fisherwoman was soaked to the skin. "You must be cold, please take my barsaati," she offered, The fisherwoman laughed, "We are like fish ourselves – so used to the water we never get cold!" They talked about homespun matters until they reached the garden. Suddenly the fisherwoman took in three or four sharp breaths and exclaimed, "What is that smell?"

The gardener smiled, "The garden."

"The garden?"

The gardener's voice quivered with pride as she began to describe the wonders of the royal garden: "You shouldn't be so surprised! You won't find a garden as magnificent as this for a hundred, maybe two hundred kos. The nobles come by from all the nearby estates to beg for cuttings and seeds from my garden. Of jasmine, and rose, and champa, kevra, mogra..."

"You sleep here at night?" the fisherwoman interrupted, holding her nose tight.

"Of course! Where else would we go? I can't sleep anywhere but here. Even the soil here is fragrant! If you like you can take a few plants home with you. The flowers will remind you of me."

The fisherwoman, struggling to breathe as shallowly as possible, teased the gardener, "Why, would I forget you otherwise?"

It had stopped raining. The gardener folded the barsaati and said generously, "It's not as if these flowers were beyond your means! There should be no formalities between us — what is mine is yours." Opening the gate to the garden she continued, "I have the Rajaji's permission. He wouldn't object if I filled your entire basket with flowers."

The moment they stepped through the gate the fisherwoman thought her head would burst. She pulled down her veil to cover her nose and mouth and softly said, "Why should we do anything to risk his displeasure? And what would *I* do with flowers?"

The gardener stared at her in surprise, "What would you do? You simply have no idea how wonderful my flowers are! Why, even the most powerful nobles drool for a single one of these gorgeous blooms. Touch a petal and the fragrance will stay on your fingertips for three days."

The fisherwoman could feel her insides roiling now. How could the gardener even breathe? It would be impossible to sleep here. She felt as if her nostrils were being scorched. Why on earth would the Raja want such a foul-smelling garden? These questions churned in her mind even as her head reeled, but she didn't have the courage to ask the merry gardener.

The gardener let them into one of the rooms next to the garden. Then fingering the fisherwoman's dripping clothes she said, "You sit here. I'll go and get you some dry clothes," and ignoring the fisherwoman's polite protests, she vanished. As soon as the fisherwoman stepped inside the room, her nausea quelled a bit. Then the gardener reappeared with a stack of clean, dry clothes heaped with roses and jasmine, and beaming happily, she held them out to her. The poor fisherwoman could barely keep herself from vomiting.

Suddenly, the gardener sniffed the air sharply and wrinkled up her nose, "What's that awful smell? Never smelt anything so offensive in this room before!" She looked around and saw the basket lying in the corner. "Why did you bring your empty basket inside?" she asked, irritated. "That fishy smell makes me feel as if my head would burst!"

What could the fisherwoman say? The gardener guessed her quandary and so quickly took the basket out herself. Then she sniffed her hands and realized that now they too had that same smell. She vigorously scrubbed her hands with sand four times.

The fisherwoman accepted the meal she was offered with apprehension. If she were to vomit now, how embarrassing it would be! Once the meal was over, the gardener took her leave and went to the room next door, and the fisherwoman was immensely relieved.

The gardener was just as relieved to get away from the fisherwoman. Such a foul stench coming from that woman's body! But of course she refrained from saying anything out of civility's sake.

In the other room, the fisherwoman was just as scrupulously polite and restrained herself equally. She kept tossing and turning for a good hour and more. In the end, she quietly tip-toed outside, retrieved her basket and lay down again. With the empty fish basket over her face she instantly began to feel lighter again. She would rather die than spend another night in any famous royal garden! She was stuck today, but never again she promised herself. Soon enough, the basket's soothing fishy fragrance lulled her into a deep sleep.

a hound's pride

May God keep the rising sun on his path, and that all will be meet. Whether it is meet or perhaps plain chance, wherever you see man, you'll find dogs, and wherever you find dogs, man won't be far off. The bond between these two has been primal and unwavering.

Once in a basti somewhere, it so happened that a wealthy seth bought a bloodthirsty Sindhi dog from a Banjara for one hundred and eight gold coins. His name was Nahar. And like his name promised, Nahar had the build of a lion: tall, strong and broad. The same tapered waist and terrifying roar. Proud ears, big, red eyes. Teeth sharp as knives. Jaw lean as a fish. Tongue red as a birbahuti bug. Soft, shiny fur. Paws like cushions. Twenty one claws. A tail round as the mouth of a pot.

The rich seth was pleased that he had found someone to guard his vast wealth just as he had wanted. Only such a bloodthirsty beast could keep this ever-inconstant and deceitful Maya safe. Why, not only burglars and thieves, Goddess Lakshmi herself wouldn't risk taking a step out of his haveli. This Nahar was auspicious for the seth. Lakshmi would be bountiful.

Nahar kept watch all night. He attacked any thief who came near and sent those who returned straight to the realm of Lord Yamraj. The burglars tried everything possible to kill him, but he never fell into their traps.

Once four dacoits came to the seth's counter in broad daylight under the pretense of doing business. Nahar noted their looks, the way they carried themselves, and he smelt their motives at once. They had barely met his wrathful gaze before they were lying dead in a heap. They had no time even to draw their weapons. Then he bit their noses off.

After that no thief or dacoit had the courage to come near.

Sethji doted on his watchdog as he would on a son. But what could Nahar do when the seth's own flesh and blood connived with the thieves? To Nahar, father and son were masters alike. Nahar was suspicious, but only for a moment. How could he doubt the seth's own true-born son? It would be a slur on his reputation! And so he got caught in their game.

The seth had three sons: two were young, and the third grown and married. The bahu was a nasty woman, the type who was always greedy for jewellery and ornaments. But in this family, such hopes were smashed since her father-in-law was as stingy as she was greedy. To her father-in-law, commerce and savings were something sacred; only wealth invested in worthwhile transactions was real wealth. Money choked up in ornaments and household goods was as precious as dirt.

Every night the seth's eldest son had to endure his young wife's shrieks and shouts. The barrage filled his ears and sent his head reeling. It poisoned his mind. Until finally one day, he did as she urged: he lured a gang of thieves into looting his father's vault with the promise of a quarter share.

To carry out the plan he began feeding Nahar sweet, buttery choorma every night exactly at midnight. Every night for the next two weeks without fail, and not a second late. Then on the sixteenth night, while petting and stroking the dog, he reached into his bag and pulled out a wire mesh muzzle and slipped it over the dog's mouth. He then bound Nahar's four paws together with a rope before the dog knew what was happening and pulled it so tight Nahar couldn't stand and couldn't make a sound. All he could do was writhe on the ground, struggling fiercely to work his way free, until he was covered with cuts and bruises. Meanwhile the thieves had dug a passage to the basement and were busy clearing out the seth's vault. Once they were through, not one screw was left. The seth's eldest son packed his bags and fled with the gang of thieves. He had arranged for four camels to wait outside the village. He gave the thieves their share of the loot and headed straight for his in-laws' haveli. His wife's face seemed to bloom in the window when at last she saw him coming down the road.

The next morning when the sethani caught sight of their watchdog tied up, rolling on the ground struggling to break free, she felt shock waves course through her body. She ran frantically towards the vault, and when she saw the passage the thieves had dug, she broke into hysterical sobs.

At the sound of his wife's wailing, the seth ran down from the sleeping chamber, two steps at a time. The worst that could possibly have happened had happened. But how, with Nahar still alive, Nahar, their ferocious watchdog? They had relied on that dog, and now everything they had was gone. That bastard must be taking revenge from a past life! Well, a dog was just a dog. What could he expect? The ingrate! Bit the hand that fed him! If Nahar had been doing his job, Death himself would have dreaded coming near.

The seth was so enraged he could have dragged a scythe slowly across the haraami's throat. But how could he when he had absolutely no knowledge of such things? He was someone who stepped around ants as he walked. There was no end to his grief at losing riches that his family had watched over for generations. That chandaal had damned the name Nahar for all time! He cursed and shouted and kicked the beast. Tears streamed down Nahar's eyes. But what could he do besides look up at his master with beseeching eyes? If it had been under his control, things never would have turned out this way. He could swallow his master's kicks and curses only because he knew ignorance was blindness. The anguish of losing such immense wealth was beyond his comprehension he knew. But the seth could have at least removed the muzzle from his face and allowed him to tell his version of events.

However, it was the sethani who turned out to be the clever one. She freed Nahar from his bonds and listened to him talk, and what she heard made her lose her mind. The seth's suspicions would not be erased. No mother's darling could even dare come near his shadow unless Nahar had somehow been in league with him. He must have known. This was the price you paid for trusting a dog. The seth again started cursing and kicking him. He spat on him. After a while, his legs got tired and he stopped. He panted, "Haraami, it's all because of you that my wealth is gone! Go, get out of my sight!"

Nahar wept tears of blood and whimpered, "What have I done to deserve this? You're unleashing your anger at your son's misdeeds on me! If a son betrays his own father, why would he stop there? The money you have lost is nothing but sweat on the brow. But the disgrace I have suffered will haunt me until my dying day. I never would have expected this from you, o master."

The sethani laughed hysterically and cried: "And you think I expected this from my son, my own flesh and blood? Human beings will cut each other's throats for money. But what did you have to gain from this? Why did you let yourself get corrupted?"

Nahar said, "I'd rather you went ahead and killed me than make such allegations!"

The seth gave him another hefty kick in the belly and shouted, "Why should we bother? If you had any self-respect you'd go somewhere and drown."

Nahar bent down before his master and said, "Believe me, I am absolutely blameless. Would you really have expected me to challenge your own son's intentions?"

"Dogs are the lowest species on earth!" the seth shouted. "Go! Get out of my sight!"

This was an insult Nahar could not forgive. "That only confirms your filthy suspicions. Now I will never go."

"There's no place in our home for a traitor like you. You'll get nothing from us, not one little crumb!"

"I don't want your crumbs. I'd rather starve to death. But I refuse to leave with your accusations stinking in my tracks."

Neither side would back down. The seth would not feed the dog. The dog would not leave. Seven days later, Nahar hadn't so much as looked at a dry piece of roti. He had grown thin and gaunt. But the seth and sethani had hearts that refused to melt.

Up until that time, Nahar had never missed a meal. He was surprised to find that fasting had sharpened his mind. As if layers of rust were flaking off his brain. So that by the seventh day he felt absolutely alert, renewed. He jumped up all at once and began to bark.

The seth and sethani were furious. But before they could even utter a word, he began: "For ages, dogs have been man's most loyal servants. And what do we get in return? Kicks and abuses. We have silently swallowed every insult inflicted upon us. We have tolerated all manner of injustice. Although I was innocent, the curses you hurled at me ripped through me like daggers. Today I am taking an oath: I will never again set foot in a man's house as long as I live. And so help me o Vidhata. I will see to it that no other dog ever takes my place, lapping at any man's heels. My entire life shall be devoted to delivering my downtrodden race from servitude."

Even in all his adversity, the seth couldn't contain his laughter. He repeated the old saying, "If dogs could ever unite, they'd have made a pilgrimage to the Ganga to bathe. If you didn't fight so bitterly amongst yourselves, the plight of your race would improve on its own."

Nahar just smiled and replied, "These stories have all been concocted by man. Cram them down your gullet and spit them out. But I'll never forget the lesson you have taught me. For this, I will always be grateful. Therefore, if I deserve any reproof, please forgive me." And with that Nahar took his leave.

Four or five days went by before Nahar felt his strength return. He had been spending his time meditating on the plight of dogs and on ways of uplifting them, when at last he knew what he must do.

Nahar was an outstanding member of the community, revered and respected. But when the others heard him speak, they were afraid. Had he gone crazy? How could they challenge invincible man? Men could get by without dogs, but dogs couldn't survive one day without men! If they started believing in Nahar's wild plan, their entire species was doomed. If they set up a separate basti just for dogs, they wouldn't even be able to protect themselves from hyenas. They would be ripped apart! And then those feasts of meat would become a distant fantasy. Why would any game dare stray close to such a basti? Living with men they had grown used to enjoying bread, butter, milk, curd, curries and sweetmeats. What would they get instead? Living with men, they had been cared for and protected. But by themselves, where would they find such protection?

The leading members of the community explained to Nahar that his interpretation of the situation was a little dubious. Dogs were meant to live with men. A course as radical as the one he was proposing would end up wiping dogs off the face of the earth. Nahar should go back and reconsider.

Nahar had thought over all these things before. He knew what the obstacles were. But if you got disheartened and disillusioned before you even started, what could you ever hope to accomplish? He knew it wouldn't be easy to rid them of habits flowing in their veins for ages. But Nahar's goal remained firm as ever: freedom, freedom, FREEDOM! Freedom for ever and ever!

He went over his ideas with each and every dog. A hundred times. A thousand times. And slowly his dedication and determination began to cut through the gauzy film over their eyes.

Soon his conviction bore fruit. The dogs established a separate basti for themselves in the middle of barren wilderness. It was only the very old or infirm who insisted on staying behind. The dogs came from everywhere. Within twelve and twelve makes twenty four kos around, hardly any village was left with a dog. The old dogs watched them go, making fun of Nahar as they stayed where they were, licking their masters' feet.

They were eleven thousand dogs in all. They had built their new basti in no time. The leaders held counsel and decided that the basti should be named after him: Nahargarh. The name spread through the wild like brush fire and was carried to the farthest reaches.

The ways of the dogs seemed to have altered miraculously, but Nahar still wasn't completely convinced. He wanted to put their comradery and goodwill to the test by taking them down to the Ganga to bathe. On the way there, not one dog barked, snapped or even growled. Men heard their approach from a distance and made anxious preparations to welcome them. And as soon as the dogs entered the bastis, they found big vats of lapsi ready and waiting. They were served on slabs of rock scrubbed squeaky clean. Each politely insisted to the others: Please have more. No, not before you. And as the journey wore on, the dogs' respect for Nahar grew. Men resented the harmony they witnessed among the dogs. At the slightest breach of etiquette or minutest lapse, Nahar would signal and the dogs would pounce and decimate the basti. It only had to happen once or twice, and after that no basti of men ever provided them a similar opportunity.

When they reached Haridwar, the dogs split up into groups and went down to the various ghats to bathe in the Ganga. Each swam across the river and back three times. But at Nahar's command, they all came out of the water at once. When the numbers were counted, not a single dog was missing. They stepped in line and marched home, their legs swinging in time. The hyenas leapt underground a full twenty four hours before on hearing rumours of their arrival. One time a pack of twenty or thirty hyenas stood there just to watch the tamasha. The dogs tore them to shreds at once. Would they be so stupid as to miss such an opportunity?

After that not a single hyena remained on that earth within a hundred kos.

The sons of man did not flee their bastis. But their fear of Nahargarh's new-found strength certainly kept them in line. They replied at once to the summons Nahar had issued, asking that two leaders be sent from each basti to meet with him.

Three hundred village elders stood on tip-toe before the assembly of dogs, hands folded in supplication. The seth and his son were in the crowd, trying to hide behind their mustaches. Nahar called them forward as soon as he saw them and might as well have slapped them on the back, "You probably expect me to be hostile or vengeful. But on the contrary, I am filled with gratitude. It is thanks to you that this basti has been established. But I have no time for idle talk. Looking after a new basti is no joke. Open your ears and listen carefully: for the next five years, all we need to eat, drink, and to keep warm will be your responsibility, and your responsibility alone. You may raise donations publicly or provide the funds all on your own. Your son has no shortage of wealth. Watchdogs have been exploited for ages and ages. And now it's our turn to receive some compensation. We need wheat porridge, gur, clarified butter, and coconut meat, served on platters big enough to accommodate five dogs at a time. Who would be better than you to calculate all this? Keep proper accounts for everything. Send us fifty servants. I suggest that all the villages take turns month by month, so that you don't start fighting amongst yourselves. And beware, the person who speaks ill of us — he will end up worse than ill."

The men clasped their hands and begged for mercy. Then they sat down together and drew up lists and schedules. Accordingly, the goods would be brought to Nahargarh month by month. No mistake would be tolerated. Or else the assembly of dogs would maim them for life.

So the men pitched in and built a separate hut for each dog, as Nahar had asked. They built a giant fort in the very centre. And they gave each dog a cloak to protect him against the cold.

The awe the dogs felt for their leader grew so rapidly in the basti it seemed to double by day and quadruple by night. However, there was one particularly severe proscription which created an absolute uproar: the dogs were forbidden from coupling with more than one chosen mate. A crisis Nahar found easy to tame with a firm hand.

He was the unchallenged ruler of Nahargarh. Disobeying his command was a crime punishable by death. It was crucial to protect the precarious foundations of a new basti such as theirs.

On every full moon he called an assembly. And on every full moon he said the same thing: "There is no danger greater than man. Put your trust in that race and they will surely disappoint you. Our strides forward here have tormented them no end. They are weaving nets of conspiracy behind their closed doors even as we speak. You can search the world over and you won't meet a creature as ignoble and ungracious as man. If he can slit his own parent's throat, what prevents him from doing away with us? It is fear that forces him to comply with our demands. It is fear that makes man our slave. If men could only unite, they could level Nahargarh in a moment. So you must be careful. Collude with them and you sow the seeds of chaos and destruction in every home."

The months went by, one after another, the end of each month bringing such joyous relief to the men on duty they felt as if they had been given new lives. During their term of responsibility they could neither sleep during the night, nor rest during the day. If a man sat idle for even a moment, the sound of a dog's growl nearby would throw him into spasms of fear.

Over time, Nahar's arrogance and self-conceit grew unbounded. Then a few of the more shrewd dogs began sending their wives to him. In the beginning, he was careful to keep it under control. But how long could that last? Soon he had grown quite accustomed to having a new dog or two each night. Then the back-stabbers started whispering in his ear. And gradually he began to differentiate between the dogs in Nahargarh. There were those on his side. And there were the pariahs.

Inevitably, the taint of dictatorship soon seeped into every pore of his body without him even being aware of it. He became increasingly consumed with the subtleties of personal pleasure, and grew blinder and blinder to the misfortunes of others. For the survival of the basti, he must remain the ruler of Nahargarh, he told himself. Why, the lives of so many were at stake! Only he could assume such a tremendous responsibility. There's no greater glory than being the leader of a hundred thousand dogs! He had not only established a new basti where there had been none before, but it was he and he alone who had united a race infamous for its petty quarrels and deadly brawls. Such vanity could crack a boulder. And here he was, a living, breathing dog. It wasn't long before his whole thinking had changed.

He would wake up in the morning just before sunrise and think to himself, now it is time for the sun to appear. Then, sure enough, the sun would peek over the horizon, just as he had willed it to. As he looked around him and noticed the small miracles of daily life – the breeze blowing through the trees, or the swollen clouds in the sky rumbling and raining – he told himself that even these forces of nature depended on him. The rivers swelled and shrank at his whim. Without his sanction, the moon would no longer shine, stars no longer twinkle, and flowers no longer blossom.

The citizens of Nahargarh were very proud of their undisputed leader. But the next year, when the population suddenly increased twenty-fold, all his grand plans were reduced to dung. There was discontent. The fifty men could hardly build enough huts to house so many dogs. They couldn't feed them on time, nor keep them watered, nor bed them down at night.

Nahar refused to listen to any advice about increasing the number of servants. What if the men began to plot against them? They would lose instead of gain. These poor, innocent dogs shouldn't even trust a man's shadow. The dogs had eaten the same sweet day after day for so long, the taste of gur lapsi had started rotting on their tongues. They wanted meat. But providing meat to so many was impossible. Nahar wracked and wracked his brain and finally came up with an idea. The drums began to beat the orders across the narrow streets of Nahargarh: No couple can have more than one pup. One pup for each family, and the rest will be used as meat. Anyone who disobeys this order will be publicly executed.

It was as if all of Nahargarh convulsed at the decree. But Nahar's trusted army brought the disturbance under control in no time. Heaps of dogs and pups lay piled up in the alleys. In every lane, steam began to rise off the warm streams of fresh blood. It certainly was an agonizing job watching out for the welfare of the basti, this was no joke.

He told his citizens over and over again – that their biggest enemy was man. It was only due to man's desperation that he deigned to serve them. He will take you down the first opportunity he gets. One of his most dependable spies brought the news that they were ready to mount an attack on Nahargarh with an army of a hundred-thousand hyenas. Divided, we'd be wiped off this earth without a trace. It was a shame that wily man could lure a few greedy dogs into such a heinous plot. If Vibhisan hadn't turned traitor against his brother Ravana, would Lord Ram have ever escaped from Lanka alive? It was the Vibhisans of this world more than man who were the real threat to the community! Nahargarh could only be saved if they watched out for those treasonous dogs!

Proclamations from their leader rang out in the narrow streets of Nahargarh every day: Beware! Man may attack at any moment! Beware! The spies may be in your own home! Beware! The worse the domestic situation became, the more proclamations were sent out. Beware! All the dogs within Nahargarh tightened their belts and braced themselves to kill or be killed.

But all this proclaiming and posturing soon became too much for a dog named Heliya. He snuck through the alleys whispering in the ears of his cannier companions. And slowly his words began to take effect. One by one, the dogs aligned themselves with another coalition in Nahargarh and began singing a different tune. Nahar's spies reported everything to him, with extra pepper and spice added. This was like a barb in his throat. Meanwhile, Heliya's numbers were increasing. Nahar had to get rid of the traitor. He was just waiting for the right moment. Luckily for him, the chance came sooner than expected.

One morning a bullock cart was seen approaching the basti carrying a bale of thorny brush. All the citizens of Nahargarh assembled at the sound of Nahar's deep roar. Nahar leapt up on the stony platform and rearing up on his hind paws, began to shout out authoritatively: "The danger we have feared so long has finally arrived! To show our invincible strength and unity, I beg of you – Bark! Everyone bark! Bark with all your might!"

The dogs began to bark so loudly the very air seemed to roil in whirlpools. Nahar closed his eyes and appraised their strength. With such sameness of purpose and overwhelming zeal, they were invincible! Nahar raised his paw for silence and the entire assembly stopped at once.

Commending them on their discipline with a nod he went on: "That human chandaal can't stand by and witness our success. He has filled his cart with dark, foul-smelling death and brought it close to us. But we must remain patient. He would like to blame us for starting an attack. But we will not react and get caught up in his game. Beware! We must not initiate any violence."

The churning-murmuring of the bullock cart drew nearer. Heliya looked over and realized what was going on. He stood up on his hind paws and suggested politely: "It seems you have overlooked one point. This is merely a heap of dry jujube branches. Men use these for fencing. This should present no threat to us."

Nahar growled loudly and then roared in anger: "Do you think I'm such a fool that I would not even recognize a threat to the basti? Am I the founder of Nahargarh or are you? Are you the one who fought to free our downtrodden race from its fetters? If it is not I who is responsible for the welfare of Nahargarh, then who is?"

Heliya had just opened his mouth to reply when Nahar raised his paw and roared to the assembled crowd: "Challenging the order at a time of crisis is an invitation to death! Bark once more! Bark! Bark with all your might!"

They began to bark so loudly it seemed as if the sky itself had blasted apart and shattered. Heliya's voice was a flute drowned out by the boom of a kettle-drum chorus.

All the dogs of Nahargarh barked away, noses in the air, while the driver smiled and coaxed his bullock cart off through the streets.

When at last the barking had died down, Heliya clasped his forepaws together and proclaimed, "It is the good fortune of Nahargarh that this danger has been averted."

Nahar twitched his ears and snapped, "Has your brain grown an extra layer of fat? You crowning fool! The danger has been averted, you say? It has only been delayed. If they attack at night there's nothing we can do to stop them. I'm going to go and assess their strength so we can be prepared. One should never underestimate one's enemy. Wait here and stay calm while I go and sniff out the potential danger. I will return in an hour. I beg you with folded hands to flush out the traitors in our midst. They are at the enemy's beck and call. Bark at such treachery! Bark as loud as you can!"

The dogs pointed their noses high as they barked and began clawing at the ground with their paws. Except for a group of a hundred or so dogs – Heliya's pack. They sat on the side, trying to contain their laughter and didn't make a sound.

Nahar ran off after the bullock cart with a flourish of his tail. What if there really was something dangerous instead of innocuous brush? The thought made him slacken his speed. Who knew what tricks man was capable of? Suddenly the memory of that night he'd spent bound up and writhing on the ground played before his eyes. Such vicious kicks! And curses unrestrained! How he sobbed and cried! That soul-wrenching hunger!

He ranged behind the bullock cart for two or three kos. The sun beat down strong on his troubled frame and set him panting. Then he ran alongside the cart for a while. Finally he decided it won't be too much of a risk, and he plucked up courage to duck between the wheels just beneath the bullock cart. The churning-murmuring of the wheels moved along in time with his feet, in rhythm with his breaths. He paced along in the cool shade, deep in thought. Over his head towered the bale of jujube brush. At a signal from the driver, the cart slowed to a stop by the side of a pond. As the cart came to a halt, so did Nahar. He was convinced that the cart had stopped because of him. As long as he remained in the shade of the cart, it didn't move one finger-width.

Then the driver whipped the bullock and the cart jerked forward and started rolling down the road. Nahar leapt up the same instant and kept pace with the bullock. Now there was no room for doubt. The cart moved only when he moved. He had never known what strength his four skinny legs possessed. Could there be any burden greater than the cart? If all the world were to stop and start at his behest, would it be a greater burden?

As they went along, the cart stopped exactly where he stopped and started moving again with a creak and a groan when he started walking. It gave the old saying a whole different meaning: The hound walks under the cart and thinks it starts and stops at his will.

At last when he was fully convinced of his powers he dashed off towards Nahargarh. All the dogs were sitting quietly, yawning, waiting for their leader to reappear. Heliya sat apart with his friends, engaged in a different type of consultation.

Nahar mounted the platform and declared: "As long as I am alive, you will have no cause for fear. With your support there is nothing I cannot accomplish. I had a good look at that bullock cart, and I must say, that contraption can't compare with my might. It moves only under my power, and halts only when I will it to. Those who doubt my word can come and see for themselves."

Heliya stood up and said, "There's no need to go there. I would simply like to ask one question. Then I will be completely satisfied."

Nahar noticed the ironic twitch in Heliya's lips and it made the blood leap into his eyes. He had to get rid of this troublemaker today and no later. Such an opportunity would never come again.

Clasping his forepaws together in supplication, Heliya went on to ask, "When you were sitting with us in Nahargarh, how is it that the bullock cart had the power to move along the road? And now that you have returned, how do its wheels continue to roll? Dispel this small doubt of mine, and I'll never question you again."

Nahar smiled derisively and replied, "What difference do your petty little questions make to me? None. But trying to mislead and provoke the citizens of our basti during this time of crisis is a heinous offense. I cannot tolerate this insurrection, not at such a delicate hour, when before us looms a matter of life or death. The smallest crack can spread and spread and break our rock of unity asunder. Instead of pouring my strength into fighting our enemies, I am wasting it arguing with imbeciles. I have the welfare of our many citizens in mind when I say I cannot afford to take this risk. How long has this insurgent been feeding you such khak? Get rid of him and all his henchmen right away. I don't want a single..."

But no one had the patience to listen to another word. They pounced on Heliya with an explosion of growls and fur and tore him to shreds. His allies met the same fate. After they had ripped through all the other carcasses, four or five dogs swooped down on Heliya's remains when suddenly Nahar roared: "Beware! If you eat the brain of this traitor, your mind will also rot. This is the most lethal kind of infection, a disease that will kill you even before you die. Beware, anyone who has even looked in its direction!" Immediately everyone drew back from the head.

And to this day, the skull is lying where it fell. Those who pass by feel tempted to taste it, but no one has ever had the courage. As the sun moves along his path in the sky, an eerie glint reflects off the skull, a glint so bright even the sun is forced to squint. And a thunderous roar rips through the sky: Beware! Beware!

a true calling

Nothing happens to a story if all you do is listen. Nothing happens if all you do is read, or memorize word for word. What matters is if you make the heart of the story a part of your very life. This story is one of those.

Once there was a bhand, one of that rare breed that devotes itself to impersonations. This particular bhand was so adept at disguising himself that next to him the real thing looked fake. He would keep a disguise on for several days, and no one would ever find him out, until he clapped his hands and hooted and hollered and went back to being his regular self. He knew a hundred different languages. He could mimic the calls of all the different species of birds and animals so well that even the animals couldn't tell that the call came from a human throat. You should have seen him disguised as a merchant, a tribal, a hunter, an ascetic, a cow-herd, or a mullah, a beggar, or Lord Hanuman himself! Anyone who saw his disguises would swear he had more than one face, and many more voices.

One time the bhand put on the disguise of an enlightened holy man. Even the other holy men were astounded – where had this miraculous mahatma been hiding all this time? And how did he suddenly show up? The bhand decided to spend the four month seclusion of the monsoon at a seth's house. Crowds of worshippers flocked from nearby regions just to gaze at his holy graciousness. It made the bhand wonder if he should stay on this path of renunciation forever. But he kept a hold on himself. He would hold forth to worshippers on the nature of the inner spirit, the all-encompassing Holy Spirit, one's dharma, moksha and nirvana, and with such intensity that his body would begin to feel as if it were melting. He had not been there for long, illuminating these spiritual matters for the seth's family, when they started to turn fanatical. One receives such blessings only after many lifetimes of austerities, thought the seth. He looked again at his own familial and material encumbrances, and his soul rebelled. One day he brought all his wealth – immeasurable quantities of gold and silver, diamonds and pearls – and laid them at the holy man's feet. Folding his hands in reverence he said, "My lord, if you would please accept the worthless offerings of your devotee, then perhaps some of the filth of my material body will wash away. These represent nothing more than the meagre flowers of my heart. After all, how am I worthy to serve one like you?"

From the corner of his eye, the bhand saw the dazzling riches, and then he looked at his guise with his soul's eye. A fierce dust storm was gathering inside his heart. He felt as if he were dangling between heaven and hell. After a few moments he opened his eyes, now sparkling like stars. The holy man smiled and said calmly, "Son, why do you insist on coating my face with your detritus? You are a family man, and I am a sadhu. If I were to hold out my hands to grab the priceless treasures you're dumping like so much gravel, it would be an insult to my vow. I am not so gullible."

The seth could never have imagined such a thing even in his worst nightmare. A man of his experience should never have made such a grave miscalculation. He was well aware of the avarice of many enlightened men. They could pull gold coins from the muck with their teeth and not feel the need to rinse out their mouths afterwards. Underneath their saffron robes, they were only the lowest of beggars wandering from village to village. The seth had reached such a resolute decision only after his heart had turned away from the material world. And now this deity in human form had ruined everything! Still, Seth-sa wasn't the sort to admit defeat so easily. He folded his hands again together and implored, "Those of us trapped in this net of materialism and domesticity become crooked, mean, and lustful, and there's no telling when we will be corrupted once more by the lure of wealth. Right now money may as well be dust for all we care, but we may not be able to remain firm in this conviction for long. You do not know the sins I have committed for the sake of wealth. Your words have liberated us. Now it's up to you to do with this wealth what you will. Let your holy hand direct it toward some sacred work and make our lives meaningful, my lord."

"And throw dirt onto my vow? No, my son, I could not accept such an offer even in a dream. The wealth should lie nowhere else but inside your safe. I am sorry."

The seth and all the members of his household stood still as statues with folded hands. But the holy man refused to relent. Heaps of priceless treasures were piled high between them. Neither side was ready to back down. In the end the holy man was compelled to adopt a harsher tone: "To whom are you bowing, do you have any idea? Put this serpent of gold back into your safe now. After the monsoon season of seclusion is over, I will do whatever you say."

The seth prostrated before the holy man and said, "As you wish, my lord."

A profound smile danced on the holy man's lips, a look as deep as the earth's core. A moment later the smile vanished. And just as time is beyond a sadhu's control, beyond a seth's control, a day passed, a week passed, two weeks, then a month, and then the holy man's entire monsoon seclusion was over. The seth was beside himself with excitement thinking that finally he would get his wish. A holy man of such divine stature would never renege on a promise, not under any circumstances. He would do whatever the seth wished. If his hands could direct this wealth to a meritorious cause, then the seth's whole life would be rendered meaningful. Just remembering all his old misdeeds set his liver trembling.

Meanwhile, whatever thoughts were coursing through the holy man's mind, only he could tell. Now that the period of his disguise was over, the mahatma revealed his secret. Slapping his cheeks and making clownish faces like any other bhand he begged: "Annadaata, if you have been pleased with the art of this poor slave, then grant a generous reward! I am a servant at your feet, Shankar Bhand!"

As soon as he had announced his true identity he clapped his armpits again, slapped his cheeks, clapped his hands. Seth-sa couldn't believe his eyes. This was a truth more terrifying than death. All his calculations had been turned upside-down. God forbid such a horrible thing should ever befall even his worst enemies! What words was he hearing from this man he had considered a god? It just wasn't possible. How could a worthless bhand have it in him to spurn all these riches as if they were dust? Astonished, he asked in a voice thick with emotion, "Is this another one of your leelas just to test me? Heavens! Better my eyes should close forever than see and hear all this."

Then he rolled up his sleeve to prove his identity to the seth. On his naked wrist in clear blue was tattooed the name: Shankar Bhand.

Instead of Lord Shankar, a bhand named Shankar! Oh what catastrophe was this? Shaking off the dizziness caused by his sudden disillusionment, the seth started thinking about the predicament he was in. Well, which saint, sadhu or mahatma can throw away so much wealth? Then this bhand was as good as any saint! Still, the shock didn't lessen. All this had happened because of the bhand. The faith of all his family members was ruined. How was this ignorant bhand able to weave such a delicate web of illusion? The seth still couldn't accept the reality. He thought it over a little and said, "You fool, I placed uncountable wealth at your feet. If you had taken all of it and disappeared I would have considered it my own good fortune. I would have counted the mala beads in your name. Now after throwing away so much wealth spread out at your feet, you are holding out your palms begging for rewards in the name of your art? I was a fool to offer you all that wealth, and you were a fool not to take it. Whatever possessed you to be so wrong-headed?"

The bhand slapped his cheeks and replied, "What seems wrong-headed to you Sethiji seems right-headed to me. While I was in the holy man's guise, it would have been an insult to those robes to be tempted by riches. For someone of my calling, taking money under those circumstances would have been wrong. I can only lay claim to the rewards my patron bestows on me. So what if you fell into deceit? I didn't. I never forgot the truth. My family has been kept waiting for four months. Lord, may you grant a reward with an open hand to a bhand such as I, celebrated throughout the kingdom!"

By now Seth-sa was back in true form. He stammered, "I'm so angry I could lash you a hundred times with my shoes. You cannot possibly imagine how much you have shaken me. Greed and renunciation cannot cohabit in the same mind. If I wish to fly to the heavens then how can I stay here on earth? Oh, once you've tasted honey, how horrible it is to gulp down dirt! I'm neither fit for heaven nor for this earth! Ask for however much you need. If my spiritual account is ruined, let it be ruined. You can ask for hundreds of thousands and I won't be taken in now. I see that I'm the one responsible for seeking out my own path to salvation, or damnation. Hurry up and ask for whatever it is you want and just leave me alone."

"Revered Sethji, the right to receive is indeed greater than the right to give. I will accept whatever you give of your own generosity."

"Look, stop playing around like this. Go ahead, I'm giving you full freedom even though you're a bhand. I'm ready to give you whatever you ask for. So ask."

"It is my dharma to ask. But in my profession it's considered improper to specify an amount. Forgive me, but I do not consider the role of a bhand any less worthy than that of a holy man."

"That's fine and good, but you are the one who set this turmoil churning inside me. Already my greedy heart is starting to waken. From those many countless treasures I had surrendered to you, I shall bestow upon only you five gold coins, whether it makes you happy or not."

"And why wouldn't it make me happy? This is as good as five thousand gold coins to me." And so saying, Shankar Bhand set off for home. Now he had his fists full of millet, salt, peppers, turmeric and coriander for his family. Clothes. Shoes. Bangles for the wife. Clay toys for the children.

After spending nine silver nights with his wife and playing with his children, Shankar Bhand went to the king's court. News of the sadhu in disguise at the seth's mansion had already reached the raja's ears. His name had spread like the wind throughout the kingdom. The raja rose from his throne and greeted him with respect. The bhand prostrated himself at Rajaji's feet and then bowed to each courtier in turn.

It just so happened that when he presented himself at court, there had been much talk about dayans and witches. When the proper moment arose, the chief minister implored the king, "May His Highness command Shankar Bhand to appear before us in the guise of a dayan. When will such an opportunity present itself again? The subject has been on our lips for the past three hours."

The other courtiers approved of the chief minister's suggestion. When Rajaji saw all the courtiers agree so heartily, he issued an order from his own esteemed mouth that the bhand appear the next day in the guise of a dayan.

A tremor coursed through the bhand's body as soon as he heard the king's order. He folded his hands in fright and implored, "I would carry out the Annadaata's command even at the cost of death, but please consider the supplications of a poor bhand. I can assume the guise of anything in this world. If I become a stone and sit on the road, no passerby would even guess this was a man. By your grace, Lord Shiva blessed my forefathers in this manner. Lord Shiva himself suggested my name to my mother in a dream. Thanks to His greatness, taking the form of a dayan is mere child's play for me, but it could cost the onlookers dear. If I am not able to take on a character completely during a disguise, then it will fail. The disguise would be incomplete if the dayan doesn't drink a bowlful of fresh blood of a human victim she has ripped apart herself. Oh Protector of the Poor, I cannot settle for mediocrity. Before I take on a disguise, and after I have left it, I am nothing but the Lord's worthless servant. But during the disguise I absolutely lose consciousness and fully enter the new existence. I am not aware of anything else. If the Provider commands I will happily put my head through a noose, but I pray to you with hands joined not to force me to take on the guise of a dayan."

Rajaji was not able to fully comprehend what his subject was trying to say. One need not possess a great deal of intelligence to be a raja. He asked in his superior tone, "Why? Why don't you want to appear as a dayan?"

After a long, careful explanation the bhand said as simply as possible, "Lord Ram only knows whose murder could take place at that time. While in disguise I won't be aware of His Highness even. To a dayan, king and pawn are equal. As it is I am a slave to your feet, but there is no higher honour than the calling of a true artist. Now please consider carefully whatever order you give, because I will be compelled to follow it through."

Like mosquitoes, the courtiers didn't need any excuse to bite. Right away one of them rebuked the bhand, "So are you suggesting that the Provider gives orders without careful consideration? How dare you!"

"How dare you!" Rajaji repeated the words of his cleverest courtier, "Are you suggesting that I haven't been aware of what I've been doing until now? That I haven't given careful consideration to my orders?"

"No, my Lord, that would be impossible. Only we foolish subjects have to stop and consider. Rulers and gods need never think over what they do. I have committed a grievous error, my Lord, I beg your forgiveness. Tomorrow will the sun give careful consideration before allowing her rays to shine? Will the clouds think and consider before raining? The flowers before blossoming? The leaves before sprouting?"

"Stop this foolish talk," the minister interrupted. Then he turned toward the raja and said, "Your Highness, this is just a professional ploy. If a bhand doesn't blow like an empty storm cloud then he wouldn't be a bhand. And this bhand is famous throughout the world. When he was at the seth's haveli, his holy man disguise reached its target like a bulls-eye from a novice's bow, and so now he thinks he can pull the same stunt here. The poor man's never been inside an elite court before. Go ahead, do what you want. We'd all like to see you rip open a heart to fill your bowl. You know very well that you won't... a man's heart isn't made of dough."

"Yes, a man's heart isn't made of dough," Rajaji repeated the minister's words. "Now you will have to come as a dayan tomorrow. If I get in your way, then you will have to rip open my heart. Speak up now, or are you going to come up with another excuse?"

"How would I dare make excuses to my Lords? If you won't listen to my pleas and warnings, then I am helpless. But tomorrow if anyone's guts are spilled, you will have to forgive the crime."

"So now you'll have the Esteemed King write out a contract?" the minister retorted angrily, "Stop this disobedient nonsense! If you don't know how to take on the guise of a dayan, then say it."

After such a shadow had been cast on the bhand's reputation how much more could he appeal? He slapped his cheeks and armpits and cried, "As your graciousnesses wish. After all, you are the Lords of the Lords."

Words fly from lip to lip faster than the wind. As soon as the whispers went around the court, everyone in town knew that the bhand was going to appear in the guise of a dayan the next day. Would fill her bowl with the blood of a man whose heart she had ripped out with her own sharp nails. The sly courtiers were going to select someone from the populace to put in front of the dayan. Everyone was so afraid even the birds didn't dare enter the court.

The next day, all the queens, princesses and handmaidens were sitting in the windows and balconies counting the minutes waiting for the bhand. The raja and all the courtiers were sitting in the courtyard anxiously glancing about when suddenly she appeared before them, hissing and puffing, her tongue hanging out of her mouth all the way to her chest. All those courtiers who only yesterday had clamoured to see the disguise now forgot everything and took to their heels as soon as they saw the dayan. A frightful tumult ensued. This must certainly be a real dayan. She had found the perfect ruse, pretending to be in disguise. Her foot-long tongue was dripping with blood. Her hair flew in every direction. Nails so sharp they could slice through a rock. That bastard bhand must have arranged for a real dayan to come. The court emptied out in a flash. Rajaji led the stampede. He stumbled and fell two or three times but he never even looked back to see how far behind the dayan was. As soon as he fell he got up and kept on running. This was the first time he had ever had to exert himself like this. He had never before recognized the value of exercise. Now he understood. He was going to go running every morning and evening. You never knew when it would be useful. He was even going to order his queens to start running.

The courtiers ran in a panic like a flock of birds scattering when a rock is thrown in their midst. But the raja's brother-in-law could not run. He just lay there sprawled out in his drunken stupor. He saw everyone fleeing and tried to move when suddenly his eyes locked on the dayan. He stood there transfixed as if his legs were stuck in quicksand.

He began trembling like a peepal leaf in a storm when he saw her long, blood-coated tongue. His own tongue shot out of his mouth in fright. After all, what did a dayan care who or what you were? She leapt on him. There was no one there to forbid this, no one to stop her. She fell on his chest. Ripped his heart out with her sharp nails. A stream of blood spurted out. Her bowl was full in no time. Then she put her mouth against the fountain of blood. Her entire face was covered in blood. Heh heh heh, she cackled. But there was no one to witness her blood-stained laughter. She glanced side to side as she gulped down the bowl full of blood. Then she began to dance, pounding her heels into the ground, dham-dhama-dham, jangling her iron bracelets and anklets.

After some time, she stopped dancing and looked around her. Not a soul in sight. Then she took off the dayan's guise to become the bhand once more. He slapped his cheeks and called out, "Annadaata, I am your poor bhand. I have performed this dayan guise at your bidding but no one has remained to see. How can you blame me? If there was any deficiency in my performance, then you can find fault. Oh Protector of the Poor, now if you are happy with this bhand, grant him a reward."

When the courtiers returned there was an uproar. The chief minister crackled like lightning, "Murderer! How dare you ask for a reward? Seize him! Seize him before he absconds!"

All twenty courtiers pounced on the bhand like hungry cheetahs and then bound him tight with rope. The raja's brother-in-law had taken all the happiness he could from this world and had gone searching for it in the next. It was necessary to experience that happiness as well. All were wide-eyed, staring at the body in fear and astonishment. Blood continued to flow from the ripped-out intestines. And still everyone was hoping the queen's brother would shake off his drunken stupor as always, get up and grunt for more wine and women. Pounce on whichever servant girl was at hand. But surprisingly enough, instead of joy in the eyes of the courtiers, there was terror.

Rajaji could not figure out what the trouble was. Why had they tied up the bhand? Why was his brother-in-law sprawled on the floor like that? Why wasn't he thrashing about as usual? Why wasn't he sputtering and groaning? The raja was beginning to get cramps in his legs from all that running. But no one even seemed to care. Not a single person came to rub his legs or massage his head.

As soon as she heard about the death of her beloved brother, the queen came running into the court as fearsome as man-slaying Chandi herself. At first the courtiers thought that this was the bhand in another disguise. But he was tied up tight. Then this must be the esteemed Rani-sa. She came close to the corpse and began to wail aloud. As soon as she laid eyes on the bhand, she gnashed her teeth and said: "I will not drink a single drop of water until I see this devil's blood fed to the dogs in a bowl."

The court was abuzz. Rajaji shuddered at all this talk of blood and corpses. His mind became a frozen blank. He signaled for his brother-in-law's corpse to be brought to the queen's palace. The courtiers all cried in a single voice: "Your Highness, disaster has befallen. And still the instigator's head is on his shoulders. Give the command and we'll tear him to shreds."

Confused, Rajaji asked, "Why, what has happened?"

"Nothing short of a disaster, Annadaata." Each courtier was anxious to curry the raja's favour. Who knew when such a golden opportunity would present itself again? The man who got himself killed was dead and gone. It was the living who had to worry. Rajaji only became more confused listening to everyone shouting out explanations all at once. He was still exhausted from his run. The cramps would come back as soon as he touched his legs. His heart was still beating too fast. As they say, no one worries about his father when at the point of death.

Finally after hearing the minister's careful explanation, Rajaji began to understand. After all, it was his responsibility to see to law and order in his kingdom. He said, "All of you are telling me to execute this bhand. Why? Where were all of you crumb-grubbers and hangers-on then? Do you really think the bhand would dare to do such a thing when he's just one man? Did every one of you run away?"

"Yes, my Lord, it behooved us to run with His Highness in order to save your invaluable life. You are our lord and master." Then the chief minister had to explain from the beginning. Rajaji was nodding his head as he listened and the ever-patient and sincere minister was explaining the matter to him once again without betraying the slightest frustration. Finally when he had understood everything thoroughly, Rajaji said, "Ah, so that is how it is. I must put the murderer to death. You don't need to explain a simple matter like that to an intelligent person more than once. And here you fools go on and on explaining every detail to me like I was a child. No, no, anyone could see that such a transgression cannot go unpunished."

The bhand bowed before the raja and, stifling his outrage, said, "O Annadaata, have you already forgotten the pledge you made yesterday? When the ruler of the kingdom himself breaks his promise, then how can he expect anyone else to follow his word? If instead of a reward I am put to death, I will comply with His Highness's wish. You are the Lord of Lords, are you not?"

Rajaji could think of no reply. He sat there, silent. And in her palace, Rani-sa had not let go of the idea that her brother's final rites would only take place after the bhand's. How could the bhand be considered more important than her brother?

Yet the raja could satisfy neither the rani's thirst for vengeance nor answer the bhand's protestations. There would be trouble if he didn't honour the queen's concerns and trouble if he broke his pledge. How many problems appear before a raja? Who could ever count so high? Not even he!

The shackled bhand asked, "And what does His Highness decree?"

But His Highness's brain was in a fog. He was unable to summon the proper reply and kept swivelling his head towards the courtiers on his right, and then to the courtiers on his left, over and over, like a marionette. So far it hadn't been that long... only yesterday, yes it happened only yesterday. In this very court the bhand had been assured that even if the raja himself came in the dayan's path, it would be understood that she could rip out his guts. How much the bhand had protested putting on the guise of a dayan. But in fact no one knew what would happen, no one imagined it would turn out this way. As soon as the fatigue in his body lessened and his heart slowed down, Rajaji began to go over the previous day's events one by one. Ah, yes, how much the chief minister upbraided the bhand for refusing. If he had disobeyed the raja's order it would have meant death. He obeyed, and now he was in trouble. The queen wouldn't rest until her brother's death was avenged. Suddenly, Rajaji grew suspicious. Looking over at the bhand he said, "But if you were going to rip anyone apart, why my brother-in-law? If you had attacked anyone else, it wouldn't have been such a problem."

"Oh Protector of the Poor, everyone ran away to save themselves as soon as I arrived. Only His Lord's brother-in-law was too drunk to run."

"So that's what it was. If only you had recognized him, then this horrible crime wouldn't have taken place."

"No my Lord, when I am in my disguise no such discernment is possible. That is why I tried so hard not to take on that guise. But no one heard me, no one believed me, no matter how hard I protested."

"If that had really been the case, you should have tried harder, or not taken on the guise at all. You should have just gone back to your village."

"I acted in error, my Lord. What else can I say?" He might have been able to press oil from a stone, but not a drop of hope from this raja. The bhand understood that it was useless to try and say anything further. He bowed once more and stood silent.

"You tell me yourself, what should I say to the Rani-sa?"

"The only answer is that murderer's death!" Rani-sa cried out. "I need no other reply. You are wasting time discussing this matter with that devil. Make haste and give the order of execution."

"But he had tried to warn us," Rajaji began to argue in an attempt to be fair, "The chief minister and even I myself ordered him to take on the guise of a dayan."

Suddenly a barber stepped forward, "My Lord, if you will allow me to humbly make a suggestion... so that the honour of your word is upheld, and Rani-sa's wish too is fulfilled."

Rajaji perked up and asked, "How would you do that? How?"

The barber started to explain with pride, "If this bhand is so eager to uphold the honour of his true calling, then why not ask him to take on the guise of a sati's sacrifice on her husband's funeral pyre? What did it matter to him that he ripped out someone's guts while disguised as a dayan? Let's just see if he can uphold the same code when disguised as a sati throwing herself into the fire."

As soon as they heard the barber's suggestion, all the courtiers' faces brightened, but Rajaji still hadn't quite figured it out. Still, he was the king. Wisest of all the wisest men in the land. The chief minister explained it all to him patiently, and finally he understood. And once he finally understood, his happiness knew no bounds. "Very good! Today you have truly rescued my honour!" Then turning to the bhand he said, "Now let's see you refuse. Your arguing isn't going to work this time. Say: are you willing or not? After that I'll give you a reward for both guises, don't worry."

The bhand said, "Annadaata, if it's theft or adultery then I worry. What is there to worry about here? All I ask is that my remains be delivered to my home and that my sons are told that in my last moments, I testified that honouring one's true calling is the highest honour of all. That way they will carry on the profession properly."

"That is all?" Rajaji asked in surprise, but the bhand said nothing further. After that the incomparable bhand did just what he said he would. Thousands gathered to see a man assume the guise of a sati. Soon, a cremation pyre of sandalwood was laid. She mounted the funeral pyre with the natural bearing of a true sati. Such was the power of her conviction that flames leapt up from the pyre of their own accord as soon as she ascended.

The sati disguise had been fully realized.

As soon as the bhand's remains were burned, Rajaji rewarded the barber with a high posting. He bestowed upon him a golden platter filled with pearls. He was pleased that the matter of avenging his brother-in-law's death was resolved without breaking the promise he had made.

The queen settled down after seeing her brother's murderer burned. And she was relieved to learn that her husband's honour had not suffered the slightest blemish.

How to compare a king's honour with the true calling of a bhand?

untold hitlers

The five were only men. Some younger, some older, all between thirty and fifty. The eldest was beginning to gray here and there, but the others had heads of hair black as bumblebees. They looked like men: eyes where eyes should be, noses where noses should be, teeth where teeth should be. Arms and legs where arms and legs should be. Copper-coloured complexions. White turbans, some old, some new. Cholas of white muslin, like their dhotis. Knotted gold earrings in their ears. Gold pendants around their necks hung from black cords. Each man spoke like a man. Each man walked like a man.

All were farmers. They worked the land and reaped the yields. The dry womb of the earth turned green with their wheat and fennel, mustard, cumin and fenugreek. After Independence, these mighty farmers had done well. They cast the seeds in the dirt with eyes closed, then gathered up the fruits. The five looked as if they had been born not of woman's flesh but from the earth's own womb. As if they had grown up and blossomed among the kareel, aak, khejari and acacia trees. As if the grass, the trees, the shrubs, the flowers were their kin.

The five were brothers, cousins of near about the same stock. They were going to Jodhpur to buy a tractor. Each had bundles of rupee notes stashed in the undershirt pocket at his breast. The heat of it made their faces glow. The roots of wealth may tap deep into the heart, but the sheen of such invisible fruit shines clear for all to see.

They stepped off the bus, hands in their pockets, and headed off, their strides long and brisk, towards the tractor showroom as arranged. If it were in their power, they wouldn't have let even their feet touch that pavement black as rot. Once they reached the showroom, they recognized the owner through the window front. As soon as their eyes fell on his shiny bald pate, they cried, "We're in luck! Om-ji himself is here today."

A blast of ice-cold air rushed over them as soon as they pulled open the door. They walked into the shop, and one sighed, "Here he's enjoying heaven, while we toil like beasts of burden."

Om-ji smiled a thin smile and said in a delighted voice, "If you want to exchange your farm for my shop, I wouldn't object."

"Hah! You'd regret it!"

"That remains to be seen."

The eldest cousin chided them, "We've only just walked in, and already you're talking about regrets. Each man must follow his own fate and do the work that suits him best."

Sitting on those cushiony chairs it didn't seem like they were sitting on anything. They poked and prodded the soft cushions two, three times to make sure the seats would hold their weight. Satisfied, they settled into the chairs, elbows on the armrests. After the perfunctory duas and salaams, one of the cousins began, "Somehow or the other, our number has finally come. We need to have the tractor today. We started out this morning at an auspicious hour. We must return to our village before the day is done. We would consider it a favour if you could arrange for it somehow."

"Every customer I meet makes the same demand. You have waited more than two years, and now you cannot even wait two more days?"

The youngest cousin said, "Two days would be too long. At this point we cannot wait another two hours. Our women have been standing at the doors ever since we left this morning, watching for our return to auspicate the tractor. Charge a little extra if you have to, but you must deliver it today!"

Om-ji smiled at their impatience, then said, "I know how you rustics are. I made sure the tractor was ready yesterday. Take it whenever you wish."

Their joy knew no bounds. It was as if they had suddenly been handed the whole world to rule! The middle cousin looked at Om-ji's head shining like the moon and said, "How could a man with such a lucky brow ever shirk his work? May you live long!"

The cousins were familiar with Om-ji. One or the other would come by from time to time to check their number on the waiting list. He became as friendly with them as business demanded. His manner was easy, his words pleasant. Every bit of him looked like it had been manufactured in a factory like the parts of a tractor. There was a bald spot where a bald spot should be, fringed on three sides with thinning hair. A neck where a neck should be. A smile as the occasion required.

He scanned the five faces before him and said, "You must be relieved. You've spent your whole day bouncing up and down inside a bus. Now sit back and relax, have some cold water," and he reached for his buzzer as he continued to make polite entreaties. A man came in at once. Om-ji asked him to bring some lassis. When the man disappeared, he began apologizing, "I will not be able to offer anything to rival what you get in your village. The milk here is water-thin. The yoghurt would turn your stomach. All you get in cities is cooled air, icy water, soft cushions and bright lights. The grandiosity of the adulterated and the ostentation of the fake. You cannot find good grain and spices at any price. I am ashamed to offer you anything at all."

One of the cousins laughed and said, "If you really mean to offer, there are plenty of luxuries to be had around here. The envy of the gods above. Otherwise, we'll just have to cool down with a lassi instead."

The hint was clear enough. Om-ji laughed loudly and said, "No, we cannot have any of that here in the store. But if you can wait till evening, I will be able to offer you real hospitality at my home."

"Your invitation alone is enough, Om-ji! Where's our tractor? Let's just take a quick peek."

"First have your lassis and then we'll go down and have a look."

"The lassis aren't going to run away, are they? The sight of the tractor will cool us down. Then the lassis will taste sweeter."

Om-ji went with them himself. The tractor stood ready in the workshop.

A blood-red Massey Ferguson, vivid as a mound of birbahuti bugs. The sight of it made them flush in their hearts. They patted the tractor and inspected it closely. Then they all went back to the office. Their glasses of lassi were sitting on the table, carefully covered.

Om-ji eased himself back into his chair and began musing, "How times have changed! There used to be just one thakur who ruled over the area. But now you big peasants have become the new thakurs. You are the ones who have really taken advantage of Independence. Where before people used to dream of having buttermilk, now they order all the luxuries as if they were water. In the old days, people couldn't even afford a plough and a spade; but now no one gives a second thought to spending thousands on a tractor. Yaar, enjoy this Independence, have as much fun as you can, don't think twice."

The fourth cousin interrupted him, "I wouldn't call that khak fun! Nothing to eat but grain and you barely fill your belly. We've suffered for a thousand generations. Now the one-eyed lady puts on makeup, and you begrudge her airs? Thanks to Gandhi Baba we actually live like human beings now. How else would our villages have got all those motors, tractors, and radios?"

"And soon we'll have to fill our stomachs just with paper notes. Before too long, we won't even be able to buy grain."

"You just keep giving us tractors and we'll keep giving you grain. Draw up a contract if you like."

The eldest cousin spoke up, "No one gives anything to anyone just like that. The water buffalo grazes only to fill his own belly. Everyone everywhere wracks his brains just to find a way to meet his own needs. One does it by selling a tractor, and another by buying it." When his words reached his own ears the eldest cousin realized his talk had gone down the wrong path, and he tried to steer the conversation back to better terrain by adding, "Still, what you say is true. Due to Gandhi Baba's grace, we're better off since Independence. Heaps of grain in every home, milk and yoghurt flowing freely..."

Om-ji, shaking his bald head, cut in, "No, not in every home, that's not true. It's only a small number of you big farmers who have all you could want."

The youngest cousin had been to college. He said, "What do you mean *all* we could want? The best you can say is that the jaws of misery's grip have loosened a little. Just enough to give us room to breathe. But happiness is still as distant as the moon."

Wanting to put an end to all this nonsense the middle cousin said, "What's the use of wishing for the moon? Let's get down to business. Take the money out of your pockets and give it to Om-ji so we can get our goods and return. We're wasting time talking."

Suddenly they all remembered why they had come. A moment later their hands were in their pockets, pulling out rupee notes, piling them on the table. A fifty horsepower foreign-built tractor with trolley, harrow and plough. A sixty-thousand-rupee transaction.

Om-ji got busy counting the money and putting it away in his drawer, while the five cousins all stood up and went down to the garage for their merchandise. The eldest cousin sent the youngest off to the bazaar for garlands, loaves of gur, rum, and bright red gulal powder. The four cousins helped to load the plough and harrow onto the trailer. They had just caught their breath when the youngest returned. They celebrated by passing around the loaves of jaggery and festooning the tractor's hood with marigold garlands. Then they painted a gleaming red swastika on the front of the hood in gulal. The youngest three were able drivers.

The day had passed quickly. The sun was just about to slip behind its western veil. From the Ajmer-Jodhpur toll gate the road looked clear, smooth and wide. The garlands fluttered in the breeze to the rhythm of the engine's roar. Sitting atop the tractor the five cousins felt as if heaven itself were gliding beneath their wheels. And the earth curving towards the horizon before them seemed punier than a coconut shell. As if the sinking sun had paused in the sky just to gaze at them. As if the thrumming wind were trying to sweep away any inauspiciousness. All the happiness in the world tossed inside their hearts. Even the long journey of the setting sun's rays seemed to be made worthwhile at the touch of the goddess sparkling in their pendants. The tractor's clanging sent birds hidden in roadside thickets and trees flying in all directions. But to the cousins, it was their own happiness taking wing.

Suddenly a shrill cry broke into their revery. They looked around, startled. A hawk was swooping down, its wings spread wide, on a baby rabbit it had spotted hiding in the brush. It seized the trembling body in its talons and soared upward, back into the sky. The cousins smiled and looked at one another. The eldest observed, "One's fate can never be postponed. It was destined that his death should take place in this very bush, by this very hawk, at this very moment." They gazed into the sky until the hawk faded away. The tractor continued to roar along the road. They were approaching a small overpass. The fourth cousin urged the driver on, "As much as we're hurrying we're still running late. So far, everything has been auspicious – there were good omens when we left the village."

A steep slope lay just ahead. As they came over the crest they noticed a cyclist riding in the distance, just a few furlongs ahead. The cyclist heard the roar of the engine and turned to look behind. A tractor coming. He turned back and began pedalling furiously. The men sitting in the tractor noticed him speed up and watched as the gap between them widened. The youngest cousin was at the wheel. He muttered, "Fool! Pedal as fast as you like, you'll never beat a tractor!" He gave the throttle a little tug, and it roared louder.

The engine's roar rattled louder in the cyclist's ears. He pedalled faster, and the gap widened again. The driver couldn't stand to see the distance between them. He accelerated even more, saying, "Little mother lover! He'll tire out in the end, let him enjoy his little triumph while he can." The middle cousin added, "You never know what's going on inside the skulls of those bareheaded punks."

The tractor was racing along by now. The garlands began flapping even more wildly. The eldest cousin agreed, "Of course he'll wear out. Why bother pulling out the speed? A poor cycle can't compete with a tractor!"

A piercing shriek struck their ears as an eagle swooped down from the sky and pounced on a mouse scurrying desperately to get to his hole underground. A moment later, the shrieks faded away. The sun was half-sunken. Now the sun would also disappear for the night. Scarlet light radiated from the setting sun, red as gulal, as if reflecting the tractor's red gleam. The brothers turned from the setting sun and looked at the road ahead. Arey! He was even further ahead! The same thought pinched all of them: a two-hundred rupee cycle against a sixty-thousand rupee tractor. No match! Does a mouse dare to wrestle an elephant?

The second cousin spat out, "If he pumps those pedals till his lungs burst, it's his family he'll be leaving behind." The fourth cousin said, "Ram only knows when he'll leave his family behind; all I can see is that he's leaving our tractor in the dirt." The youngest cousin eased out the throttle a little more.

The tractor was brand new. It wasn't good to race along at full throttle.

The cyclist looked back. He had quite a lead now. And his exhilaration made him pedal even faster. His feet were spinning round and round like reels. The cycle slipped down the road as easy as water down a mountainside. As if the cyclist had turned into a whirlwind, or even that he were riding a whirlwind.

All eyes on the tractor were rivetted. Quite a gap lay between them now. And it was growing wider. A foreign tractor. Worth sixty-thousand rupees. Festooned with marigold malas. And a two-paisa cycle! A college punk. Head bare. Wearing knickers.

A sharp gust of wind snapped one of the garland threads. The garland began to flap around. Doubling up, unfurling straight. Another garland snapped. The tractor driver felt every thump of the marigold garland on the hood like a thorny cane beating against his breast. He ground his teeth together and pulled the throttle out to the limit. The tractor catapulted forward like a shot from a cannon. The sound of the revving engine echoed in the air. The sky that moments ago seemed to be gliding beneath their wheels now seemed to be rising higher and higher over them.

The gap began to close. Even more. Ah, now they were really close.

The world seemed to grow small as a coconut, reduced to two little dots. The tractor. The bicycle. A sixty-thousand rupee machine. And a two-paisa piece of junk.

As it happened, two army trucks came bumping down the road from the other direction just at that moment and the tractor was forced to slow down. The cyclist saw his chance and clipped ahead.

The middle cousin said, "These city punks are worthless! Taking advantage of a chance like that!" The eldest cousin said, "If the poor thing wants to show off for now then let him. How long can he carry on like this? He's bound to run out of breath. Pagla, squandering his energies like this. Once his internal piping starts sagging, he won't even be able to do it for his woman. Were such drives meant to be spent on a cycle?" *

Now that the road was clear the youngest cousin opened up the throttle. Like gunpowder suddenly touched with a spark. The tractor was like a duststorm trying to catch the wind. And gradually the gap began to diminish.

The cyclist heard the tractor just behind him and looked around. He snapped his head forward in a fury. And his feet began to spin like reels. They became speed itself, speed and nothing else.

Now he had begun to sweat. He was the fastest cyclist in all of Rajasthan. And yes, he was also a man. Arms where arms should be, legs where legs should be. Breath where breath should be. Dreams where dreams should be. He had been working out on his bicycle sixty or seventy miles a day for the past two months. If he came first in the All India Bicycle Championship next month, then he might get to go to Paris. He felt confident enough after two months of dedicated training. But today's little contest would prove it for certain. He clenched his teeth and poured all his strength into spinning the pedals.

He went to college with a young woman who had fallen in love with him the first time she saw him race and proposed to him herself. But he had not been able to reply with a forthright "yes" or "no." They kept meeting and talking and spending time together, and once they had begun to know each other in their souls, it became clear what they must do. He had promised to marry her as soon as the All India Championship was over. He had been raised in tight circumstances. And she had grown up in a house of plenty. But they lived only for one another. They ate as if with the same mouth. And on their priceless wedding night the moon would smile on their bridal bed.

Suddenly her face appeared before his eyes. As if she had turned into the breeze to watch the race. His vigour increased tenfold. As if his feet had grown wings. What power did that lifeless tractor have compared to the shining image of his beloved? The cyclist pulled further and further ahead. Before long, the distance between them had doubled.

Now the tractor was at full throttle. They could do no more. Their insides started writhing. The whistling wind was being swallowed up by the roar of the engine. Their reign over the world had been wrenched from their hands in a dash. The new tractor shot down the road like a cannonball. It looked as if a whirlwind had taken over that bare-headed boy's feet. His beloved's face shone before his eyes. The distance grew and grew. His lungs didn't quaver, and his breath didn't break.

Half of the marigold garlands had snapped and fallen. But what could the cousins do?

No one can see what the ephemeral future holds. Suddenly the feet fast as a whirlwind were spinning emptily. The chain had come off. Still the boy didn't worry. He figured his feet could match the tractor's speed. Images of his beloved's face surrounded him. There could be no greater power than this in the world. He stopped the cycle and quickly dismounted. He leaned the bicycle on the kick-stand and patiently began putting the chain back on.

Slowly the distance was decreasing. The air could not contain the tractor's roar, nor the five cousins' happiness. Well, who knows when luck will smile on you? It didn't matter how, but this sixty-thousand rupee matter of honour was saved. If people want to deceive themselves into believing in fraudulent victories, then who would stop them?

The tractor's roar sounded closer. It was taking much too long to get this chain back on in the flurry. Before long the tractor was right there. And still he had confidence in his strength, and the power of his beloved's face before him.

The tractor roared past. All five cousins shouted out words typically human as they sped by. A flock of crows began cawing overhead as if in one voice. The voices of the humans couldn't be heard above the cawing of the crows and the roar of the engine.

The tractor was already one or two farm-lengths ahead when the cyclist got the chain back in place and started off again. Four of the cousins turned back to watch him. They thought to themselves, the bastard was just pretending his chain had come off! Maybe the race was too much for him.

But the chain was back on and he had turned into a tornado again. The distance between them slowly began to decrease as he came closer and closer. The scenery was beginning to merge with the darkness. The four cousins were straining to watch the boy behind them. He was gaining ground!

Now it was an all-out race. The tractor couldn't go any faster. They gnashed their teeth. The red of the tractor began to dissolve into the fading light. The youngest cousin asked, "Where is that haraami now?"

The fourth cousin said through clenched teeth, "Looks like he's going to pull ahead."

"Hah! Even his father wouldn't have dreamed of it!" As he said this, the youngest cousin heard the hawk's shrieks, then the mouse's squeals, echoing in his ears in turns. After a moment the shrieks were in one ear, the squeals in the other, and they wouldn't stop. It seemed as if the entire universe were about to rip apart. The tractor's roar got swallowed up in that echo.

A whole different world was glittering in the eyes of the cyclist. Everywhere he looked, images of his beloved's face were twinkling – in the soft scattering of stars, in the trees and shrubs, in the sand dunes, in the tractor's trolly up ahead. Today would be the test. If he could get ahead of the tractor, then he would get married as soon as possible. Tomorrow, if she agreed. If not, then the day after. Or the day after that. Whenever she wanted. Why wait to pass them? All the world was in the palm of his hand. The warp and woof of golden dreams were being woven before his eyes.

Meanwhile, the hawk's shrieks and the mouse's squeals were smothering every particle of air. The four cousins shouted through clenched teeth, "That bare-headed dogale is making us lick the dirt off our turbans!"

Then they came up with a new plan. "Make the tractor swerve as soon as he gets close. What will the little haraami have to say to that…" The hawk's shrieks and the mouse's squeals had found a human voice.

And meanwhile the images of his beloved's face began to glow brighter and brighter. Each image became more and more distinct.

Now he had moved up, beside the trolley. The shrieks and squeals hid themselves in the driver's head and assumed a posture of silence.

The next moment the speeding cyclist crashed into the tractor. Lightning flashed before his eyes and the lights of his beloved's face extinguished one by one. The tractor's rear tyre passed over his bare head, mashing it into chutney. The rest of the faces were snuffed out.

A human voice hissed once more in the wind, "Mother lover, he had nerve trying to overtake a tractor!"

The youngest cousin had been to college. He pulled the tractor over, grabbed a bottle out of the sack and said, "Let's give the poor guy some rum!" Then he went over to him, walking on two legs like a man. Opened the bottle above the cyclist. Emptied half the bottle of rum into the boy's mouth. Then he broke the bottle near the boy's head and ran back to the tractor. The tractor roared as he took off. The women must be standing in the doorway waiting for them. How happy they will be to see them!

Human laughter echoed in the wind.

A picture was left behind them on the road, waiting for expert appraisal. Brain-white smudges on a blood-red background. Shards of broken glass. A man's dead body. White shorts. Bloodied sky-blue undershirt. Mashed dreams. Streams of love. The painting wasn't bad.

But... the paintings of the two World Wars, pictures of Hiroshima, Nagasaki, Vietnam, Bangladesh... those are the true masterpieces. Compared to this one, those are so much more refined, so much more complex and nuanced. This one doesn't quite compare. Still, considering it was done by a band of rustics, it wasn't bad.

Yes, the five were only men. Each man spoke like a man. Each man walked like a man.

two lives

May the Bodiless Adehi Anang, the deity of love grant each and every one of us two lives to live. Starting with two bastis, twelve and twelve makes twenty four kos apart. The baniya seths in these bastis were famous throughout the land for their stinginess. And in those two bastis lived two moneylenders, both the same age and of the same social standing. Even though they lived far apart, they were good friends. And as fate decreed, they just so happened to tie their wedding turbans on the same priceless night, each leading a breathtakingly beautiful bride around the wedding fire at the same hour and planting his pearl in his bride's oyster at the same precious moment. Overwhelmed by their good fortunes, they took a hasty but heartfelt oath that regardless of which of them had a son and which a daughter, they would join them together in matrimony. The said offspring were hardly wishes in their mothers' wombs and already their futures had been arranged!

The two seths were so engrossed in their friendship and their money-making that they never paused to consider what games nature might play. Nine months later, at the exact same astrological juncture their wives gave birth to two girls. One of the seths — a man as true to his word as to his greed — tampered with the truth. Instead of scraping the winnows to announce the birth of a girl, he proudly rang the bell-metal and sent the barber across the desert to his friend's basti to announce that his wife had given birth to a son. Inside the havelis of both seths, loaves of gur were distributed in celebration.

At first the mother thought the whole thing was just a little joke between friends. She naturally assumed that the truth would come out in its own good time. Until then, what was the harm in pretending? After all, she thought, in the innocence of childhood, what does it mean to be a girl or a boy? Such differences reveal themselves only when the cloak of puberty is pulled away.

But intentionally or not, the father made no effort to clear up the misconception. He raised his daughter like a son, dressing her up in dhoti and angarkhi, a cummerbund around her waist and a colourful tie-dyed pagdi on her head. In the beginning it all seemed quite charming and comical. But he didn't stop the farce even after their daughter started to grow. The mother's head started to ring in foreboding. She tried warning him by gently teasing, "Why are you pretending that you can't see what's going on?"

At this the seth began to stammer, "Can't see what's going on? *I*, who apprehend realms from the highest to the low?"

His wife slapped her brow in mock incredulity, "You apprehend realms from the highest to the low and cannot see the bloom of a girl's adolescence through boy's clothing?"

The seth grew evasive, "When would I have time to worry about such trivial matters?"

"Trivial matters? Giga's father, what kind of madness is this? The girl's ready to have her palms stained yellow with turmeric, and you call it trivial?"

"It's not as if I'm preventing the marriage from taking place. I had thought it all through better than anyone could. Had the whole thing arranged even before the baby was born."

"And see what happened when you had it all so well thought through!" the sethani retorted, "Really wonderful! How do you expect a girl to marry a girl?!"

"Why? What's there to getting married? You do it and it's done. What's more important is the promise that was made. If I've given my word to someone, I will not go back on it even on my last breath."

The sethani rolled her eyes. He wasn't joking! She might as well be trying to get him to see the sun shining in the sky. Do such things need explanation? She stood there mouth agape. Being patient would only make matters worse. She braced herself and began haltingly, "My dear, just how do you intend to make up for a deficient marital bed with a promise? Think about it a minute. I've kept myself from interfering all these years because I assumed that you were joking."

"And have I ever done anything to warrant interference? Listen, we're going to get dowry wealth beyond belief! I'm going to lead my son in a wedding baraat that's the grandest you'll ever see. After all, a man can't go back on his word, can he! Why should I have to suffer a loss due to some glitch in nature?"

The sethani was now caught in sandy straits. Was her husband putting her on, or would he actually go to such lengths not to break a promise? She realized she couldn't let the matter just hang there, neither up nor down. Much better to have it settled. She erupted, "To hell with your gains and losses! How will our daughter ever regain what she lacks in a marital bed arranged by a father like you? Did you include that in your calculations?"

The seth answered arrogantly, "Well, why not? Savvy daughters-in-law wait eight, ten years patient as can be for their husbands to return from distant lands. And women who wind up with husbands that can't do the job figure out some way or other to fill their wombs. And girls who become widows in childhood figure out a way of getting by. What's meant to be will be. What is in her destiny is not ours to control. As they say, if you want to sleep with covers on, you have to pull up the blanket yourself."

At this point the sethani realized that her husband was not jesting. He wasn't going to undo a single knot in the web he'd woven. A hazy image of her daughter's face swam before her eyes and her voice choked as she spoke, "This is the daughter we gave birth to. How can we just tie her up in a bundle and let her rot? Married to a girl, what's a blanket and what are covers? I never would have agreed to this."

Irritated, her husband interrupted, "And when did I ask if you agreed or not? I am fully capable of taking care of this matter. If you start sticking your nose into everything, I might as well not exist. I'd rather die than go back on my word. Anyway, don't tell me you don't know how seths compensate for a deficient marital bed! Don't start playing the idiot now. How do you think your father's name has carried on? There's not a soul around who doesn't know. I had my eyes wide open when I gulped down that fly."

She never expected such a gibe to come from her own husband's mouth. As soon as she heard him, she shut up, lips sewn tight. So everyone knew. It felt as if the blood in her veins had frozen still. Her mother running after every man in sight, her impotent father concerned only about his accounts, her mother getting so carried away that she stopped bothering about caste, high or low, started parading around with a chamar – an untouchable! It was true, he was good looking and well-built. Everyone noticed, but who would ever acknowledge out loud that the sethani was his spitting image? The same face, the same way of walking, talking. Suddenly the seth had taken the lid off of that simmering pot of secrets and scorched her. Faltering, she said, "Do as you like."

The seth never expected his erratic arrow to hit the target so squarely. The whole matter was cleared up in one quick shot. And as luck would have it, the marriage proposal arrived at his house the very next day at the auspicious hour prescribed. He gladly accepted the proposal. But the mother felt something eating away at her insides. Still, she didn't open her mouth, didn't utter a word. Now it was all left to her daughter's ingenuity and her karma. Lord Ram only knew what was in store for her.

But her daughter was utterly naive, unaware of her body, her adolescence, ignorant of her karma. She had been raised all these years like a son, and she considered herself one. So even though she didn't know the real meaning of marriage, she was thrilled at the news. As soon as she was married, she thought, surely whiskers would start sprouting from her cheeks! Her fingers itched to twirl a big, thick moustache. It made her mother burn with grief to see her daughter's innocence.

One day a neighbourhood girl her daughter's age happened to come upon her while she was bathing, and the whole travesty was laid bare. All these years the girl had believed the seth-sethani were dressing up their daughter as a boy to avoid the evil eye. But when they started making such elaborate plans to marry her off as a groom, the dike of her patience burst. The neighbour followed the daughter upstairs and started explaining, "Look Jiji,..."

The daughter interrupted the girl before she'd even begun, "*Jiji*? Why? Every day you have addressed me as a brother and called me Bhai-sa, then why suddenly start with Jiji today?"

The girl laughed, "What do you mean why? If you are like my elder sister, then why should you get upset if I call you Jiji? Silly, you are a girl, and girls don't go around dreaming of becoming grooms! How long do you plan to parade in this masquerade when you don't have the manhood where it counts?"

"How long do I plan to parade around like this? All my life! What's wrong with my manhood? I've got on a dhoti and an angarkhi, and a turban sixteen hands long!"

The girl smiled smugly, "You can wear a turban sixty hands long and still not have what it takes to be a man. You should refuse to go along with this wedding. Your young body is longing for a different sort of coupling. You put two girls together, and how are you ever going to work the clay? You're old enough to understand this simple fact of nature I should think."

But the seth's daughter did not understand. She frowned and said, "You must be jealous of my beautiful new bride. You just can't stand to see me happy, can you?"

The neighbour put her arms around the girl and said, "Whatever are we going to do with you? Some day you'll run square into it and then you'll see.

But then what good would it do to understand? I know how eager your father is to lay his hands on that dowry, but are you sure your mother has never tried to explain all this to you? I'm surprised she has gone along with this."

The innocent girl blurted out, "I'm going to ask my mother right now. She never keeps secrets from me."

"It would be better if she didn't," the neighbour agreed and went on home, while the seth's riled up daughter ran to her mother. "Ma, today a girl I met started saying the strangest things, that I dress up in men's clothing but I'm not really a man. I shouldn't even listen to her, right? You never keep secrets from me, Ma. Be honest with me: she's lying, isn't she? I told her to her face that she was just jealous of my pretty wife."

Her mother turned away and brushed the tears from her eyes. Her voice quavered as she answered, "You think I'd keep such a thing secret from you? Oh, that brainless girl was just teasing you."

Hearing this her daughter grew strident, "I won't listen to another word she says, no matter how much she taunts me. I'd go ahead with this marriage even if I was a woman and not a man. What's important is how we feel in our hearts. When two hearts meet, why should it make a difference if they're both women? They should still be able to get married."

The mother answered slowly, "Your father says the same thing."

Her daughter jumped up happily and started dancing around, "And surely my bhayji knows a thing or two!"

So it was settled. She had a question to ask her mother and she had asked it. Why hang around any longer? She gave her turban a quick toss and with a jump and a jig, she ran off. The mother choked back her sobs and stood there mute and as still as a statue of stone.

The next day when the seth's daughter saw the neighbourhood girl, she gave her a good talking to. She hadn't been born so unlucky that she'd get caught up in such a whirlwind! She thumped her chest and said, "Even if I were a woman, I'd show everyone that I could marry a girl. And we would not be a mote in each other's eyes or anything!

The other girl hadn't yet had a child, but she had got married the year before. She burst out laughing just to hear the girl's innocent chatter, "Looks like there's hash in your drinking well. Silly, if two millstones start grinding together, it doesn't matter how long they're at it, they can't make flour. There are some jobs only a pestle can do."

"And what's so great about a pestle? Millstones feed the whole world – they turn grain into flour, split lentils for dal."

This time the girl couldn't stop herself. She clapped her hands and cried out, "Now just be sure you two don't get left behind when it comes to splitting lentils!"

Watching the neighbour's hysterics the seth's guileless daughter became embarrassed. She tried to laugh along and asked, "Why, what's there to splitting lentils?"

The neighbour hid her smile behind her veil and said, "You'll understand for yourself when the time comes."

"You already know all there is to know about such things, do you?"

"Well, we can't really compare your situation to mine."

"Yes, it would be like comparing the life of Raja Bhoj to Gangau the oil vendor's. We are going to get more dowry than all your ancestors put together could ever dream of!"

The neighbour wasn't offended. She pinched the other girl's cheek lightly and said, "Why are you bringing our poor ancestors into this? I don't think there's anyone who could ever make you understand."

As it turned out, the seth's daughter couldn't understand anything on her own, and didn't have anyone to explain it to her. The closer the hour of the wedding drew, the higher the waves of her happiness tossed. Every day she and the men in her family went to one feast after another. Then at last they all gathered together for the wedding procession: a baraat of seven horses, eleven camels, and twenty ox carts, all decked out in the most splendid finery. The groom's father headed the procession on a brown camel followed by the groom in a carriage driven by a pair of Nagauri oxen. And before long the baraat arrived at the outskirts of the bride's village. They broke open a ritual coconut at the village limits. Then they offered refreshments for the groom. And finally the pair took their seats on the wedding mandap at twilight. The two linked their soft hands in hathleva as man and wife. And the moment the two palms touched, it was as if lightning coursed through their bodies. Two strangers had now been joined in lifelong union.

The turbaned groom was sitting on the flower-strewn bed, lamp still lit, waiting to see his bride. Late in the night he heard the rustling and swishing of the bridesmaids' gowns and the jingling of anklets out on the terrace. The bride stepped into the doorway of their rooftop bridal chamber, her veil pulled down low. The groom felt buds blossoming in his heart.

The bride stopped in the doorway and refused to take another step, so her friends gave her a firm push inside and locked the door behind her. The bride walked towards the nuptial bed with the slightest of steps and sat down beside him. He folded back her veil and looked into his bride's face. Her face glowed like a moon emerging from behind the clouds. The groom's happiness filled every nook and corner of the room. Stroking her soft cheeks he murmured, "I'd heard people talk about your looks, but I never dreamed you would be this beautiful."

The bride's rosy lips parted, and in a honeyed voice she said, "Take a look at yourself. Next to you, I'm plain as water."

The two continued to gaze at one another, drinking in each other's winsome spirits. The women standing outside the room got tired of peeking in through the cracks in the door waiting for something to happen. The only heat they could see was coming from the ghee-fed clay lamp. Perhaps once the thirst in their eyes was quenched the hunger in their bodies would awaken!

The next day in the bridal chamber the same thing happened. Outside, the women's eyes felt as if they were turning to stone, and still they didn't get even a glimpse of what they were here for. Their tender calves started cramping up, and so one by one they went back downstairs. Modesty, well that certainly had its place. But what modesty was there in this? The couple had ruined two precious nights in a row! And they weren't that young. Was there any limit to the thirst of the eyes? Whether you look at each other for a moment, or sit gazing at each other the whole night until your eyeballs burst, it's all the same isn't it? Well, each to his own way, each to her own thirst.

The bride had arrived at her in-laws' house, and still her bashful groom had neither become emboldened nor changed his ways. His mother was as worried as ever. This most extraordinary marital arrangement was giving her constant shivers, despite it being the hottest month of the monsoon. And here her husband just slept on beside her, snoring away. Ram only knows where her sleep had flown off to. How those girls must struggle with the hostile night! Once their bahu realized the truth, she'd be devastated! Their own innocent child understood nothing at all. Went off to get married so happily. You could argue that their daughter at least had walked knowingly into that bottomless well, but their poor bahu went in blind.

Meanwhile the ghee-fed lamps in the newlyweds' bridal chamber were glimmering shyly. The bride, playing with the tail of her groom's turban, murmured, "It's so stuffy in here. Take off your turban and relax while I fan you."

She began to fan him with a beautiful, brightly coloured fan. Her groom started to protest, "But a pagdi is a man's crowning glory. Lose that and his masculinity goes limp. If you insist, I'll take off my shirt."

The bride continued to fan her groom with quick movements of her delicate wrists while he began to untie the laces of his angarkhi without the slightest hesitation. The bride looked down at his newly bared chest, and before she realized what she was doing she started screaming, then fell down on the bed in a heap. Half-conscious, she mumbled, "You are a woman! What kind of revenge is being sought from a previous life?"

The groom's delusion received its first scorching, and the entire sequence of the travesty began flashing before her eyes as if painted on a story board. Now she understood what her neighbour had been trying to tell her. How delusion can make a man deaf and blind! He doesn't see a thing, nor hear. All that happens is merely an image he sees against the screen of delusion. Truth, well truth has no place at all in his world.

And now her eyes burned to see the truth after all these years. Dejectedly she stripped off her pagdi and her angarkhi and threw them down. She stripped her bride of her clothes, and couldn't stop staring at the reality of the situation as it appeared before her in all its nakedness. Why in all these years had she never been able to open her eyes to the truth? Their bodies were made exactly alike. The bride was unconscious, lying there on the bed like a big pink fish. And here was this other big fish, awakened and standing beside her. The universe must never have seen such a spectacle!

And who knows why, but the one decided she would wake up the other, and she started shaking her and saying over and over: "Open your eyes! The spell has been broken. I have committed a grave sin against you, and so it's up to you to decide what punishment I'm to receive."

After more urging and shaking the bride came to. She looked around her dazed, and then suddenly jumped to her feet with a start. They both looked so alike they could have been cast from the same mold! They kept staring at each other in disbelief. The one called husband again admitted her mistake, saying she'd only feel at peace once she'd received a proper punishment. After all she was the one who had invited all this trouble, while the bride had walked into the fire unknowingly. She had been deceived. There was no punishment severe enough for this.

The bride was gentle-hearted and wise. She knew that one of the greatest punishments a person can ever endure was to realize one's mistakes from the depths of one's heart. She knew right away that her "groom" hadn't understood any of what had been going on. And even though she insisted it was unnecessary, the groom finally started telling her whole life story. How her father had begun weaving this whole dark web of delusion out of pride – so he could keep some flimsy promise – and out of greed for dowry. How her poor mother had tried to fight it, but couldn't get her way.

The bride listened to the whole story in silence, and then gently said, "I've only had to endure the pain of this delusion for seven days. But you've had it burning inside you all these years. You have suffered more. We have both been struck by the same bolt of lightning. So we should pay for this misfortune together."

"But I was the one who played the part of the groom. So it's my fault. You were cheated by my hand…"

The bride interrupted, "You were cheated equally."

"No, I will not achieve mukti from this sin even after I am dead."

Stroking her groom's cheeks the bride softly said, "Now when you speak of mukti, you have to include us both in that release."

The other's eyes filled with tears. "If I'd been aware of what I was doing when I got married, then there'd be no trouble attaining mukti. But I can't stop feeling guilty about how I deceived you. Or I'd have shown the world the best possible marriage between two girls that anyone would ever see!"

The bride said soothingly, "Nothing has been ruined yet. We'll just have to find a path to happiness that's our very own. I mean there's nothing special in a man and a woman getting married. Watch the sun rise in the east every day, and it's wonderful. But if it were to rise in the west one morning, now that would be something to talk about."

Then she fetched her trousseau, and pulling out one of her new outfits, she began to dress up her groom in ghaghra-odhni and chunari. She adorned her with her best jewellery, lined her eyes with kohl, put a tiki on her brow. The two looked at each other, incredulous, glowing with joy. The bride leaned over and kissed both her groom's cheeks to ward off the evil eye, then said in a voice tender as a caress, "From now on, you are Beeja, and I am Teeja. We are lucky to have been touched by such an unlikely turn of fate. I don't want to hear you speak of remorse ever again."

Beeja couldn't stop gazing at herself in bridal attire and murmured, "Am I dreaming?"

Teeja took her in her arms and said, "Silly, no one can ever have witnessed a reality like this before!"

The darkness of night scattered and the sun rose in its appointed place. But when the door to the newlyweds' room opened, a sparkle struck the seth's eyes so bright it blinded him. He knew the truth better than anyone. Yet he stood there dumbfounded as if he had no clue what was going on. Then suddenly he lunged towards them like a rabid dog, "Why are you dressed up this way? Don't you have any concern for our family's reputation or my honour?"

Hearing her father shouting and stammering, Beeja couldn't help laughing. "Bhayji, all these years you've been deceiving me. And so there were things I wanted to ask you. But now I have nothing more to ask, and nothing more to say to you."

The seth stamped his foot and spat out, "You shameless creature, what do you think you have worth telling me? I absolutely forbid you to dress up in women's clothes like this!"

Her mother heard the commotion at the door of the bridal chamber and came running. She hadn't slept a wink the whole night. When she saw her daughter dressed in bridal finery, she writhed in pain, as if her whole body were alive with scorpions. It was harder to grieve for her daughter seeing her dressed this way than if she had died. They had fed and nurtured this ugly truth for so many years in secret that she couldn't bear to have it out in the open now. She looked up and saw her daughter's lips part as if to ask a question, and she rushed to her, hugged her close and sobbed, "Don't ask anything more, please don't ask! I pleaded and pleaded, used all my wiles, but I have had as little say in this whole matter as you. And yet I stand here before you with hands folded, begging you not to put a curse on your father!"

At this a smile rippled across Teeja's lips, "All you are concerned about is a curse? Don't worry, she's not going to start putting curses on anyone, and neither am I. On the contrary, we are grateful to you that you have given us such an invaluable lesson of life as a parting gift."

The seth didn't stop to think what he was doing, he just lay his turban at Teeja's feet and started spluttering, "Bahu, my honour is in your hands. However you do it, just ensure that your husband takes off those confounded women's clothes at once and starts dressing properly like a man again."

Teeja laughed as naturally as a bud coming into blossom, "You still refer to me as your *bahu*? You talk of honour and dignity! I don't understand how you could think that your honour could be saved by some flimsy little garment. And what would it mean anyway to save your honour? You've had your way all along. Now let us do what we want. All we ask is that we may reveal your deception and treat it instead like the blessing it is."

This was all the seth needed to start showing his true colours again. His eyes turned blood red with rage as he shouted, "In this house, my word is the only thing that counts! If you want to start doing what you want, you need no longer consider this your home."

At this Beeja spoke up, "I don't think this haveli can be our home any longer. Give us your blessings if you wish, but we're leaving. We cannot stand to breathe another lungful of air here any more."

Suddenly the seth realized what was really at stake. He started sputtering, "If you want to go, go. But I'm not giving you a single cowrie shell from that dowry! Don't you dare think you can count on that."

He was boiling over with rage, but his daughter couldn't help but laugh, "From now on, the only thing we will count on is ourselves. Why are you getting yourself so worked up over nothing? We don't need even a blade of grass from all that dowry and jewellery. If it wouldn't shame you, we would walk out of here stark naked."

At this, the seth dropped all pretense of paternal care and spat out, "This was bound to happen. So now you're going to start running around naked, are you? Well, you are the only one who can answer for your actions, but that jewellery belongs to me. And if we hadn't raised you this far, could you have even dreamed of such treasures?"

"Well, congratulations bhayji on having all your dreams come true!" said Beeja. And with that Teeja and Beeja began to peel off all their jewellery. They'd been so pleased to see each other so gaily adorned that they'd forgotten about the ornaments. When the sethani saw Teeja unpinning the chains of the gold rakhari from the crown of her head, her heart overflowed. She began to sob, "Please don't remove that symbol of your blessed union, the ornament of a happily wedded wife!"

The seth's greed knew no limit. But if truth be told, this greed was outweighed by concern for his haveli's reputation. When he saw this reputation, built up over generations, being demolished by his daughter's hand, he completely lost control. His wife's chatter made him furious. He gnashed his teeth, "What does this rakhari have to do with a happily wedded life? The poor don't have money to buy gold rakharis, you think they don't have happy unions? Under no circumstances am I going to let her have a single nail from this place."

Both girls were smiling as they took off the rakharis and handed them over. For the first time in their married life, the sethani lashed out at her husband.

"Have you been bit by a rabid dog?" she hissed.

The seth thumped his chest and roared, "If a rabid dog's bitten anyone, it's them, but you can't even see it! If they want to spit at all this gold and just walk away, then let them!"

At this point they couldn't stand to take another breath of this filthy air. They walked out without another word. But the mother was still acting the old part, from the heart. She thought maternal love was all about the quantity of tears you could bring to your eyes. She sobbed, "Daughter, but where will you go?"

Beeja took her time replying as she walked away, "Wherever fate takes us."

This kind of gossip travels faster than a racehorse, faster than the wind. But the people in the basti acted so deaf and dumb they might as well have stopped up their ears with oil. Whenever someone would begin whispering, someone else would instantly put a lid on it. After all, who isn't naked beneath their clothing? And anyway, who would ever have the nerve to bring up a matter like this? The elite are different – their rocks float. You can live without the sun, but you cannot live a second without the goodwill of the seths and moneylenders. The neighbours would just turn away, scratching their heads. Who would take the lead in being any different? No one had even heard of such a thing before, but they kept silent. Only those whose heads itched to be beaten dared open their mouths. Everyone went along pretending they knew nothing.

But when they saw the seth's son dressed up in women's clothing walking out of the haveli with his new bride, they could have fainted. If Bhagwan hadn't given them eyes, would they have ever seen such an outrage? Now how were they to swallow this stone? How to make an elephant crawl through the eye of a needle? Not a mouth opened to speak, and yet the gossip was churning the very air, so hot it boiled. Until every detail spattered and spilled over. The wasps' nest had been stirred. Crowds came buzzing in thick and fast from every lane to gather in front of the haveli: A union between two women! Arey, two girls have gone and married each other! It's a slap in the face of manhood! A precedent like this will be the death of the whole community. Might as well paint the sun black with tar. How did the seth manage to suppress the truth of those curves all these years? What bigger deceit could there be than this? And if it cannot be sorted out, who will respect the panchayat's authority henceforth? You can't expect a python to fit inside a pocket.

Before they knew what was happening all the members of the panchayat had gathered around the two girls, hurling threats and abuses from every direction, "We warn you not to take another step until you have settled this matter with us. If women start marrying women, what will men do? Start searching for mice holes?!"

Teeja snapped back some retort that got lost in all the hubbub. All around them rang shrieks and shouts that justice be served. Finally Beeja raised her hand for silence and at that, the members swallowed whatever it was they were about to say. When it had finally quietened down she said, "There's no need for any case to be made on our account. But if you still feel justice must be served, let me go to the haveli. Wait here. I'll be right back." With that she started walking towards the haveli. The crowd let her pass.

When she returned a little later, she was holding a scarecrow in her hands. The same pagdi, the same angarkhi, the same dhoti. She went over to Teeja and set to digging. The crowd stood there taking in the tamasha as she planted the scarecrow in the ground right there in the centre of the basti's chaupaal where everyone had gathered. The tail of the turban trailed onto the ground. A nose like a pakora on its clay pot face, with an impressive moustache to match. Then she stood up and announced, "If you are afraid of this moustached scarecrow, then I am afraid of you moustached men. You are older and more worn out than he is! We are on our way – I'd like to see even one of you mother's darlings stop us."

Her performance mesmerized them so thoroughly that every man in the crowd saw his own image in the scarecrow. Every member of the panchayat sat staring at the clay pot face, trying to make out his face in it. No one even looked up to see where the two girls were going. And once the two were out of sight, the men saw the scarecrow laugh at them in derision. What was he laughing at? What nerve that scarecrow had to dare to laugh at the acts of men! He had insulted them! The clay pot face started rattling around inside their heads. Then suddenly something snapped and the crowd jumped up as one and smashed it to smithereens. The lucky ones managed to capture remnants from the dhoti, the angarkhi and the pagdi, while the unlucky ones walked home empty-handed. It made them all feel better to have lynched that mighty scarecrow. Then each of them headed home and roared at his wife like a lion returning to his lair.

Beeja and Teeja put their arms around each other and walked beyond the village limits. Green fields spread out all around them. There was millet growing in the fields as high as they stood tall, rippling in the breeze, and vines stretched along the border fencing. Even the smallest shrubs and kareel bushes were covered in a mesh of green. Clusters of white clouds in the sky floated aimlessly above them. Whichever way they turned they saw nothing but the earth's most exquisite finery. Nature's darling daughters were finally seeing nature for the first time. Gambolling like deer they bounded up a pretty hillside. They skipped and twirled in their exhilaration and when they reached the top they began spinning and whirling round and round. The little playhouses in the basti far below may well have been a flush of pox for all they cared.

Dark clouds began to gather around the hillside, sending down wreaths of rain. Thunder began to drum joyously on every side as bolts of lightning flashed through the sky, clamouring to see the lovers' faces. Beeja wiped the rain from Teeja's face and laughed, "The lightning has been so thirsty for a glimpse of us it couldn't wait any longer and swooped down to earth! I don't think we're helping by keeping ourselves curtained in these clothes!"

Beeja played along, saying, "Why do we need to then? Poor, thirsty lightning!" and as soon as she took off her angiya, more lightning struck, as if it had been thirsting for eons and eons even while travelling amidst the rain-bearing clouds. Once it glimpsed the lotus flowers of their bosoms, its fervour abated somewhat. The nagaara drums thundered out their joyous beat once more – dham-dhama-dham.

Before long the lightning flashed again and lasted several moments. The lovers came together like velvety red birbahuti bugs and lost themselves in an embrace, drinking in the ambrosia of each other's lips as if they could flow into one another. As the rains pent up in the clouds released themselves, so did their ardour gradually slacken. The hillside's lifeless existence had suddenly been rendered vibrant and meaningful. Now there was a new spark in the flash of the lightning.

The two girls finally came to and started putting their clothes on. The thunder grumbled and rumbled louder and the lightning flashed brighter as if irked to see them getting dressed. And the thunderclaps just sent them back into each other's arms.

They skipped down the hillside in the rain feeling light as petals. Showers of happiness rained down all around them. Satiated, replete, the earth stretched out her limbs to let herself soak up the sacred love of the clouds. Only when they reached the foothill did they realize the heights to which they had ascended in their love. If there was any truth in this world purer and more sacred than the water in the clouds above, it was their profound love for each other.

But human beings can't live in this world on love alone. And these two lovers were girls. They wanted to set up a new living order in defiance of the men in the basti. This was as easy as wanting to overturn a mountain. If it were possible, they would never even turn their heads in the direction of that basti again.

Beeja and Teeja walked on, talking, joking, laughing, and before they realized where they were going, they had arrived at the steps of a haunted baori. Darkness had begun spilling onto the earth. It had stopped raining, and they paused to wring out their soaked clothes.

The desert called and whistled. The baori was deserted. A hundred and twenty eight spirits had taken over this step well. Come nightfall even the birds were afraid to fly over it. People said anyone who had even dared to approach it was never seen again. Those in the area stayed a kos away even on the brightest of summer afternoons.

The two sat down on the edge of the baori. They were much too engrossed in their conversation to bother about being afraid. Above them, a sliver of a moon was playing hide and seek in the clouds. Beeja said, "The moon hid from you and whispered a secret in my ear. If you give me a kiss, I will tell you what it is."

Teeja teased her back, "And if you give me a kiss, I won't ask you to tell me the moon's secret."

"No, you'd really like to hear it."

"Then why ask before telling me?"

"The moon keeps pestering me. He doesn't understand why I'm spending all my time gazing at his funny face, and not at the one glowing beside me."

"You're lying. He said this to me, not you."

The two beautiful moons turned to each other and were lost in a kiss, when suddenly a deep rumbling voice startled them, "I knew you would come here."

They drew apart and looked all around them. A man stood before them glowing with an unearthly white light as if he were made of moonlight. He laughed, "Today our abandoned baori has been blessed. I'm surprised that you two weren't afraid to climb up to this haunted step well."

They stood up and Beeja softly said, "We're afraid of humans. But why should we fear spirits?"

Hearing this, the chief of the spirits began to guffaw, "You are sixteen out of sixteen annas right! If it weren't for the misdeeds of wicked humans, we wouldn't have to suffer such an incarnation. So we take our revenge by giving a good scare to the ones we can scare. We loathe to even hear the name of man. Take what happened today, for instance: those chandaals did everything they could to harass you, right there in the town centre."

Teeja blurted out, "But how do you know?"

The spirit explained, "The news of your marriage reached our ears from the lips of men. Why would we be less keen than anyone else to see such a tamasha? We all sat there watching the whole drama, completely invisible to the eyes of men. We watched you two fall in love. And we were the ones who created all that hubbub with the scarecrow so you two could get away. Otherwise you think those savages would have let you go? I went along up to the hillside just to make sure no one bothered you."

Hearing this, Beeja and Teeja both shrank back in embarrassment, which only made the spirit laugh harder. "You weren't ashamed to be cavorting around before the thunder and lightning, so why be embarrassed to hear me speak of it? Seeing your love for each other has made my existence meaningful. I am the chief of all these spirits. You can live here without fear. I'll build an ikthamba mahal near this baori which will be the envy of kings. Even if the royal treasury runs dry as an owl's run, your wealth will never see an end. You'll be granted every wish, big or small. The happiness I've experienced gazing upon the purity of your love is a gift that cannot be repaid. Women will be welcome to your mahal. But I won't let even the shadow of a man touch you with his gaze. Now all there is for you to do is enjoy this magnificent single-pillared palace."

The spirit chief gestured for them to look behind them, and when they turned around, the Ikthamba Mahal sparkled and glittered before them. Such intricately carved jaalis to peer through, such splendid jharokas to gaze out from! A gentle light glimmered from within, while outside a nearly full moon stirred the air with its cool light.

They never imagined that their love would earn them such a blessing! They walked into the palace dumbstruck. A courtyard of saffron. Vermilion walls. Beds of lotus petals. Mattresses of rose. They began swinging on the swings of happiness. Rosier than the kumkum red of wifehood, the two lovebirds were so absorbed in their embrace that they had no care for this world or the next. Well, what can compare with losing oneself in the primal pleasures of Lord Kamdev?

Finally their trance broke and they came back to consciousness. When their eyes met, they smiled at one another. Beeja murmured, "The spirit chief's life has been made meaningful once again." And then without thinking what she was saying, Teeja added: "And along with him, all the gods in heaven have assured their immortality once more."

At dawn when they emerged from the single-pillared palace and saw the sun rising, it seemed as if its tender rays were emanating from the petals between their thighs. From that night on, the sun abandoned that old cave where he had always risen from, and until this day has been rising from this new station. Every happiness in the world became eager to settle into the bed in the Ikthamba Mahal. All the thirst in the universe was contained in this one thirst of theirs.

A fortnight of bliss skipped past in a heartbeat. The spirit chief made sure they lacked for nothing. One day he said to them, "You may have forgotten about the rest of the world in all your happiness, but the rest of the world hasn't forgotten you – not even for a moment. You can go to your village without the slightest fear. Don't worry, there won't be any danger: I'll be with you every moment. The women in your village are of course free to come here any time they like. Even the sun fades when he's alone. And the moon too begins to wane."

"But there are two of us!" chorused Beeja and Teeja.

The spirit chief couldn't help smiling. "But you two are as if one. And when in bed together, you merge so completely that you threaten to disappear!"

By now shorn of all shyness and restraint, they started giggling so sweetly that even the spirit chief's smile seemed vapid in comparison.

The two flitted off like butterflies circling about here and there until they reached the basti of men. The same enclosures of walls and fences. The same hen coops in the name of huts. Each with his own boundaries. His own hearth and his own fire. His own flames and his own smoke. The same teeth-gnashing, This is mine, not yours! You... You... You... ! Heaps of garbage. The race for happiness, with bankruptcy peering over the shoulder. The sighs of tauba, tauba, hoping for a child. Stinky diapers. Filth everywhere. Quarrels and strife in every home.

How could they have spent all those years in this hell? How had they grown up here? Today it made them nauseous just to think about it. Akh thhoo! But wherever they looked, the people in their village were absorbed in decorating their aangans with red and yellow alpana patterns, painting happy pictures on the walls, singing songs at festivals and preparing savouries. Swinging on swings, singing and dancing. Oblivious to the filth around them.

This time when people saw the two arrive together, not one person stepped forward to see that justice was done. Instead they slammed their doors shut in fright. Every heart in the basti trembled in fear of the spirits of the baori. Why, those ghosts could wring your neck whenever they wished! And we all know how dear our necks are to us. Who else could those two goddesses get along with but ghosts? At last they had found some company worthy of them. Anyone the two met just turned their heads and quickly walked the other way, their tall lathi clubs trembling in fear.

Beeja's father was sitting poring over his accounts when he saw his daughter and daughter-in-law coming up the walk. He nearly fell over. When he stood up he was trembling. The end of his dhoti came untucked. He brought his palms together and begged, "I am ready to return all your jewellery and all the treasure from the dowry – with interest, if you please – but I beg you to have mercy on a pathetic soul like me."

Beeja came up to him shaking her head in disgust, "We don't want any jewellery or anything else from that dowry. We only came to visit. We don't want so much as a blade of grass from this house."

"Why wouldn't you want anything?" the seth asked, spit flying from the corners of his mouth. "You are my daughter, aren't you?"

"I am your daughter, that I know. I've also known a father's love. And if you ever mention that dowry again, I'll never set foot in this house for as long as I live."

Her father didn't know what to say to this. He joined his palms together again and started stammering, "Now you have a regal palace to live in. Why should you be troubling yourself travelling back and forth like this again and again? Just say the word and we will come there."

He did not mention his fear of ghosts. His daughter was utterly disgusted. Talking to him made her feel like she was standing neck-deep in a faecal swamp. She turned and left. Teeja, who had even less reason to be there, turned around with Beeja and walked off.

Guarding the end of his dhoti, the seth scurried after them, "Daughter, you are leaving without seeing your mother? The poor thing keeps crying so hard she's starting to go blind."

Beeja didn't break her stride as she called back, "Send her there to meet us. She has nothing to fear," and started walking even faster. So Teeja was forced to run to keep up with her. She read the crests and troughs of Beeja's mind without her having to say a word. Once they had passed the village limits, Beeja made a face, "When I get home, I'll bathe with rose water. That will make me feel better."

Teeja teased, "Why? How can rose water compare with our sweet breath?" and she put her arms around Beeja. The peacocks began to call and do their elegant mujra curtseys. The frogs' trr-trr ribbed the air. A skit of leaping gambolling deer suddenly stood stockstill to peer inquisitively at their embrace. Pigeons began to flit and strut, lost in their happy cooing. Then the crickets' endless chirping sprinkled magic dust everywhere. It seemed as if all of creation had found welcome release through this novel embrace.

Before long, the quiet solitude of their Ikthamba Mahal began tormenting and calling them. They started to run back as fast as their legs would carry them, wanting to leave the hellishness of that filthy village far far behind.

The next day just after sunrise, Beeja was startled to hear someone pounding nonstop at their door. She shook Teeja awake, threw on her clothes and thudded down the stairs to pull open their sandalwood door. Her mother stood there in the doorway with her cousin. Beeja hardly had a chance to open her mouth before her cousin started teasing, "Even married women don't sleep this late!"

Beeja's eyes still had a touch of sleep in them. Paying no attention to her mother, she rubbed her puffy eyes and said, "So aren't we married women?"

Her mother and cousin were so awestruck and mesmerized by the Ikthamba Mahal that it seemed four times as wondrous to them. Now they believed all they had heard. But how ever did they do it? Only people with ghosts at their beck and call could live in a palace like this! They had rehearsed so much to say, but not a single word came to their lips now. As if they were two spiders caught in a palace of gold.

The sethani looked all around her, entranced, and then at her daughter, as if she were in a dream, "I can't believe you are the girl I gave birth to."

Beeja laughed, "That's something only you and the midwife would know. What else can I say?"

The cousin began to get irritated with the sethani's chatter. She reminded her quietly, "Isn't there something you came here to ask?"

Teeja reproached them sweetly, "Otherwise your trip here would be worthless, is that it?"

Beeja started bustling around excitedly, serving them an assortment of delicacies. Afterwards, she had them lie on the bed of gold to nap while Teeja and Beeja sat down to eat.

Then Beeja went to look in on her mother. Mother and cousin were lying there back to back, fast asleep. They had tried as hard as they could to keep their eyelids open. But how long could they, on a mattress so velvety it would turn even a wounded man's moans into snores? What were two exhausted women to do?

Come early evening they started awake and looked around them. Even a king would envy such grandeur. It was painful to take in such a fantasy with eyes wide open. The sethani whispered to her niece, "You have to tell them why we've come. Otherwise how will they ever know?"

The cousin sighed deeply, "Those big, important men would swoon to see a palace like this. I don't give it a thought or even see what's around me."

The four sat for a few minutes chatting about this and that. Then their cousin gathered her courage and began, "Hardly three days had passed before everyone in the region knew about your Ikthamba Mahal. News like that doesn't need repeating to be in the air. If our men weren't so afraid of ghosts, there'd be a battle as grand as the Mahabharata to win your hands in marriage. Even the Raja was all charged up for battle, and then turned right around in his tracks. If the lord of our kingdom himself had to back down, then who else would possibly have the courage? Big or small, young or old, deep down inside everyone in the kingdom is riled."

Teeja interrupted, "But what harm did we ever do to anyone?"

This time Beeja's mother answered, "You couldn't have done anything more harmful than this! Your relationship has been an affront to all men."

Beeja looked at her cousin and said, "We can't do anything about that."

Her cousin added the next link to the chain of conversation by insisting earnestly, "Yes, you can. That's why we are here."

The lovers patiently heard what she had to say. She carried on, "Your wedding was a farce. You are both so untouched, even a drop of a man's sweat hasn't come near your shadow."

Teeja suddenly exploded, "And we won't ever let it!"

"No, my little one, we women don't even dare to dream of such a thing. A woman can get by without water, but not without a man's sweat. Your father has received many marriage offers for you both. The richest young men of the region are ready to marry each of you on your own. You must cast aside your hollow pride and set yourselves up in a proper household. Look after a family. May you bathe in milk, bear sons and keep the lineage vines growing. Your father is beside himself all eager and ready to give away twice the dowry for each of you."

Teeja smiled, "We're already showing you the fruits of those lineage vines you say should be maintained in our name. Those vines should be dug up and pulled out right from their roots. That would be the best thing for us. The only possible response to your idea is to laugh."

The mother's face fell. She turned to Beeja and asked, "And my daughter, what do you want?"

"Why would I want anything different? The next time you think of coming all the way here to give us advice, please don't bother."

When she saw the fire in her daughter's eyes, the mother's insides could have collapsed. The thought of the spirits around the place made her hair stand on end. She looked up at her niece and quietly said, "It's getting late. We should be off." The niece stood up and they left without another word. They'd had enough of this fantastical single-pillared palace. Beeja didn't even bother to see them out.

The next day there came the same insistent knock at the door. Beeja was in a flutter as she ran to open it. There was her cousin, standing alone, head bent low.

Beeja exclaimed in shock, "Last night I dreamed I saw you standing in this doorway exactly like this. I gave you a kiss on the cheek and you ran away. I called and called after you, but you didn't look back. Now let me try to kiss you and see how you run..."

Beeja was smiling as she leaned over to kiss her left cheek. Suddenly tears began to stream down her cousin's eyes, and seeing them Beeja's smile faded. She held her in her arms and asked, "You didn't want me to kiss you? All I..."

At this her cousin began to sob aloud. "You think that would upset me? No, your kiss has only freed the tears I've been holding back all these years. I've gone over it in my mind a million times and more, and still I cannot understand how you two found the courage to do what you've done. I am unable to look at the two of you together. I didn't get a chance to talk to you yesterday when I was with Mausi. So today I've come back by myself."

When she saw Teeja her heart flooded over again. Looking back and forth at the two lovers' faces made her break into sobs. What better way to get rid of stored up grief than by crying? Every tear is filled with the bitterness of an ocean. Once the tears stopped, she began disgorging all the bile stored in her heart, saying how happy she had been as a newlywed bride to move into her in-laws' house, even as she was sad to leave her parents'. But that long-awaited wedding night everyone calls priceless turned out to be absolutely bankrupt. He was a man, but didn't possess an ounce of manliness. Her in-laws knew this, but arranged for the most lavish of wedding processions anyhow. They thought perhaps the touch of a virgin bride would put back the spark in him. His vigour would return. But there was a flaw in their thinking, and the one who had to endure its repercussions was his innocent bride. When his powers failed him, his crushed ego would enrage him so he would start biting her all over her body.

She lifted her clothes to show them: her back, breasts, arms, bottom and thighs were swollen and blue with bruises. She had gone to her mother and father crying and hysterical; it made no difference. Those high-standing families can see nothing but their honour; so who will ever draw back the curtain and reveal what's been kept hidden? How many days had she spent living under the tyranny of her father-in-law and brother-in-law? She had to do whatever they asked of her. How long can a sheep be kept safe in a cheetah's lair? When her husband found out, he didn't say a word. Just focused more and more on his work. Business had really taken off since the marriage, so everyone was happy with the bahu's arrival.

Finally Beeja broke her silence. She sighed, "And so you were also supposed to be happy with this arrangement?"

"What recourse was there?"

Teeja asked, "Are you happy now?"

"Yes, I was for a while. But then when I saw how you two stood up for yourselves, it has all become unbearable for me once again."

Beeja started talking quickly, "There's no reason now for you to go anywhere else. If the three of us stand together, who is going to go against us?"

Her cousin shook her head, "Oh ho! I didn't come here to stay. No, my head feels lighter just to be able to sit and cry. I won't be able to leave my in-laws' home until the day of my cremation. They have lakhs worth of property. Cattle and milch cows. Seven three-storey havelis. It's not so easy to stop thinking about all that. I haven't conceived yet. But once I turn over an heir to them, I'll have some peace and quiet. My younger brother-in-law has brought me here. I have to go back the day after tomorrow. But I'll never forget what I owe you. You do not know how much it strengthens me to see your courage and happiness. But I certainly don't have what it takes to start living here with you."

She had so much to say, and now the words wouldn't come out of her mouth. Her throat felt clogged. Her eyes filled with tears. She wiped them and after a few moments continued, "Yesterday you served me separately. But today I want to join you. Maybe if we fill our bellies off the same plate, I'll share a little of your steady hearts too."

Teeja tried soothing her, "You've had a steady heart all along, but the spirits of samskara just won't leave you be."

As soon as Teeja uttered the word "spirits," the spirit chief spontaneously appeared before them. Their cousin wasn't frightened. Instead she looked at his glimmering form in wonder. "And why was I called?" the spirit chief asked.

Teeja burst into laughter. "You weren't the spirits we were talking about. You are the eternal, invisible light of the future. Still, it's a good thing you are here. We are able to wage this battle only with your strength."

The spirit chief looked down, "Don't overdo the praise, it embarrasses me." Then he looked up at Beeja's cousin and said, "I've heard your tale of sadness. Now return happily to your in-laws' home. Your husband's virility will be returned to him. And your father-in-law and brother-in-law will no longer be able to touch you even with their gaze. Your womb will swell with the fruit of your husband's line and you will give birth to five boys, each one a veritable Pandav."

Her joy knew no bounds. Teeja saw this and said, "Don't let this happiness carry you away!"

Beeja turned to the spirit chief, "You do this kind of job as well?"

The spirit chief answered with pride, "There is no work we are unable to perform."

Elated by the thought of this previously inconceivable blessing, the four sat down together to eat. Soon Beeja and Teeja walked with the cousin to the village limits, and on the way they kept reminding her to send word of how things were turning out as soon as she arrived back at her in-laws'.

On their way back, Teeja noticed how pensive Beeja had become. She asked, "What are you thinking about? Tell me."

Beeja stopped. "It's true, I can't keep anything hidden from you. This is something we need to think over. I'll tell you when you can give it your full attention."

Teeja's eyes blinked in astonishment. "What's happened to that brain of yours? Why wouldn't I give my full attention to anything you have to say?"

Beeja turned to look deep into Teeja's eyes and asked, "Didn't this blessing my cousin was given make you think of anything?"

Teeja drew close and murmured, "You've been thinking the same thing I've been thinking, but it's probably not worth considering. We have nothing to be unhappy about."

"Nothing to be unhappy about, that's true. But that blessing she received has started eating away at my insides with that same old feeling of regret. All you've got to do is say the word, and you can free me from the taint I have acquired from deceiving you."

"But I've never considered you tainted."

"I know, but how can I shut my eyes to its blackness? Eyes closed, the stain just becomes darker. No, quite the opposite, it keeps spreading. You won't even agree with me on this one thing?"

Teeja began to squirm in Beeja's arms. "If I were to agree, would that change the fate of our happiness?"

"You think we have arrived at the ends of happiness?"

"I do think there is a limit to happiness, and this is it."

"Oh ho, that line is still far, far away!"

"Those are the tricks illusion plays. But if you really believe it, then go ahead and ask for the boon yourself."

Beeja dropped her arms and moved away. Making a show of sweet-tempered anger she scolded Teeja, "You still aren't listening to what I'm saying. *You* have to be the one to ask for the boon in order that the taint on my soul be washed away."

"But I don't want to be a man, not in this lifetime or in any other. You were the one who was raised to be a boy. If you want it so much, I won't stand in your way. We'll see what kind of chashni the syrup of this relationship forms."

Teeja wouldn't agree no matter what. And so in the end, Beeja had to do the honours herself. She was filled with the desire to become a man – her fingers still itched to twirl her own moustache. All these years she had worn men's clothing, and now she was going to become a real man!

When the Ikthamba Mahal came into view, they saw the spirit chief standing in the doorway. Beeja couldn't wait another second. She ran ahead of Teeja and wasted no time in asking, "Can I have the same blessing that you granted my cousin's husband?"

The spirit chief spoke loud enough for Teeja to hear, "Why not? I didn't want to bring up the matter. But if that's what you really want, there's no limit to the blessings I can bestow."

Teeja started to blush. She looked down at her feet and started scuffing them on the ground, saying, "What's the rush? Today let's just satisfy this union's every last wish."

The spirit chief laughed, "Since it seems you like your old arrangement so much, I'll grant you the chance to reverse the blessing. If Beeja tires of being a man, all she has to do is make a wish, and she will be a woman again."

Beeja was so close to having her fantasy realized that she snapped, "Why on earth would I want to be a woman again after it has been so difficult to become a man?!"

The spirit chief promptly responded, "As you wish."

Just at that moment the stars began to prick the reddening sky in melodious little twinkles. Teeja looked up and said, "Tonight the night is mine. I won't let you sleep a single wink."

Beeja responded instantly, "You're going to have to keep up the vigil every night after this, remember."

"I won't have to think about anything else after tonight."

Beeja had heard Teeja clearly enough, but she still didn't understand. They closed the door and went to the rang mahal, their anklets jingling. Teeja was in a special hurry tonight. Beeja had barely untied the first strap of her angiya and Teeja had already taken all her clothes off. Teeja grabbed Beeja's hands and asked, "How come you're moving so leisurely tonight? Usually you are the impatient one!" Then the two rose-coloured chakwa birds came together, shook out their feathers and scarcely took a breath the whole night. Teeja hoped it would never end, while Beeja couldn't wait for the morning to come.

Despite what each of them wished for, night ended at the appointed hour and the morning came just when it was supposed to. The pleasant morning sun felt fiercer than usual against Teeja's eyes.

As the sun rose, Beeja felt a tingling sensation coursing through her body. Her chest had become completely flat right before her eyes. Hair started sprouting on her cheeks and above her lip, and it tickled! Beeja reached down to scratch between her legs and discovered it was true – she had become a man. Beeja's whole body was covered in dark, curly hair. He ran excitedly to a mirror and looked himself up and down, overjoyed. It scared him to see the curly ends of his own moustache. But how could he be frightened of his own reflection? Such a thick moustache was meant to put the fear in others!

He noticed his pagdi, angarkhi and dhoti hanging on a peg on the other side of the room and ran to them. He had been dressing himself up in men's clothes for so long that he lost no time putting on the dhoti, with a three-corner tuck and no less. He slipped on the angarkhi and wrapped the handsome pagdi around his head, leaving a proud tail that swung down to his knees. He looked around with a self-satisfied expression. He didn't see Teeja anywhere. She should be here right now. He began wandering around the Ikthamba Mahal, yelling her name. Finally Teeja called back, "I'm bathing, don't come in!"

Why this modesty suddenly? He set off in the direction of her voice. He shoved back the ruby curtains and stepped inside the bathing room. Teeja doubled over and screamed, "Turn the other way while I put on my clothes!"

Her husband backed away in surprise and asked, "Why now? You were never this shy in front of me before."

"Before things were different."

"But we are the same. Come out and see my new look. My moustache, my turban."

"You had a turban before."

That peeved him. "What are you doing just standing there spouting nonsense? Come out here right now."

Teeja emerged sparkling and freshly adorned. She looked him up and down. So handsome it made her heart lurch. Curly moustache. Strong physique. The hair on his arms and chest cobra black. Teeja looked away and said, "I'm tempting the evil eye. I better wind a black thread around your wrist to ward off trouble."

Teeja looked different to her husband today. Such intoxicating eyes! Such luscious vitality! Every pore in his body burned like live cinders. He could scarcely control himself as she stepped close to tie the thread on his wrist. He felt her fingertips brushing his arm and felt an electric current racing from head to toe. He took Teeja in his arms and coaxed, "All my past due accounts can be closed today."

Teeja bowed her head shyly and said nothing in reply. Ram only knows where he got it in his head to start talking like this. He added expressly to vex her, "I'm going to burn so bright we won't need a bedroom lamp tonight."

"Stop!" Teeja interrupted. "That's enough. You've become a man late in life – first go learn some gentlemanly manners."

"It looks like the sun will never set today."

"Today it will set early, just be patient. You look worn out, have something to eat and take a short nap in the bridal chamber. I'm just going to take a walk around the basti."

"You stayed up just as late as I did last night, so why all this now? You're going to leave me here and go off on your own?"

"What, you want me to come with you? Modesty and self-respect may mean nothing to you, but my brain isn't off grazing. How can we disregard our worldly duties?"

Her husband leered at her, "It seems I'll have to show you how to attend to worldly duties."

The next instant he had lifted Teeja up into his arms. Teeja kicked and flailed, but he wouldn't let her go. He laid her down on the rose-strewn marital bed and had his way with her.

Darkness began gathering before Teeja's eyes, and the next moment a new light radiated from the blackness. It was as if lotus petals were being torn up and scattered, torn up and scattered, even though nothing at all had happened. Teeja felt as if an entire universe were contained in her body. Before long the two uncoupled and they both lay there, barely conscious.

The husband didn't even open his eyes, just grunted, "All this time we've been writhing away uselessly."

Teeja rolled over to face him, "Uselessly? Why uselessly? I'm never going to forget those moments we had together until long after I'm dead."

That night, the same rounds. And in between rounds, a thought flashed in the husband's mind – how powerful men are compared to women. Such virility! How could those fragile creatures ever compete? Man certainly had superior strength.

That very night the husband's seed took hold inside Teeja's womb. By the early hours, the two were so exhausted they felt torn limb to limb and finally they fell into sleep's soft lap. The next day the sun was well past rising when the husband opened his eyes. Sunlight streamed into the room and awakened in him a certain pride in the fact that it was only masculinity's brilliant glory the sun donned each morning before his journey across the sky. A woman was only his shadow.

Previously, the two of them had owned the Ikthamba Mahal jointly. But Teeja better not think everything would be just as it had been before. He decided the matter must be brought out into the open here and now. He was so impatient he couldn't even wait for Teeja to wake up. He started shaking her violently, shouting, "Teeja, Teeja!" until she startled awake.

She rubbed her eyes and yawned, "Why did you wake me up out of such deep sleep?"

Her husband's ears were incensed to hear such a question coming from his wife's mouth. He chided her in a harsh voice, "You can sleep anytime you like, but right now there's a question that must be answered: Who is the master of the Ikthamba Mahal? You or me?"

Teeja didn't understand what he meant. She wasn't able to respond and instead just sat there mute. Her husband couldn't conceal his impatience any longer and repeated the question. Teeja stared at his moustache as she spoke, "Why do you need to start making distinctions about who is the master of the house and who isn't? We both live here together."

"I didn't ask who lived here and who didn't. Just tell me clear and simple: Who is the lord of this property?"

Teeja answered slowly, "The spirit chief."

At first her response knocked him off balance, but a moment later he recovered himself enough to shout, "Why are you talking in circles? Just tell me clearly: after he handed this place over, who became the owner? To whom does all this vast wealth belong? To you? Or to me?"

Teeja felt her mind empty out. How could he change so drastically in just one night? Beeja had never asked these kinds of questions before. It was only after Beeja had turned into a man that everything spilled upside-down. But now if she hesitated in answering him, things could get worse. "You and I have equal rights to this property. But if there's a doubt, why don't we go to the spirit chief to clear it up?"

Her husband's veins became taut in anger. "Are you trying to bring in the spirit chief to frighten me? You know very well he'll be watching out for you and not for me. What would he get by deciding in my favour? Never in my wildest dreams would I have imagined that you'd have such a wily scheme up your sleeve."

"Is that what you think now?"

Her words were like a spark on dry tinder. The curly moustached man started sputtering with rage, "You will see I'm no less mighty than your beloved spirit chief. I'll set up a new kingdom for myself. Amass countless wealth. Start a four-branch army. Build a fort from the strongest mortar. There will be hundreds of queens like you in my pleasure palace to dance attendance upon me!"

Teeja cut him off, "You haven't even broken your night's fast and already you're jabbering such nonsense!"

She got off the rose-strewn bed and left the sleeping chamber without another word. This Ikthamba Mahal was wearing on her nerves. How did all this mine-yours talk spring up between them overnight? This was the same old despicable path of their ancestors. It led into the same quagmire. Just stepping into a man's skin Beeja's unblemished soul had turned black as the world turns dark after sunset. Even bathing in the pool of nectar didn't ease Teeja's mind. The sun has no more control over an eclipse than the moon. Staying here would only give rise to more bitter quarrels. It would be better to go stay with her cousin-in-law. Why should she wait for her to send word? Maybe if she stayed away a couple of days, they'd both cool off a little.

She got ready to go and had just opened the front door of the mahal when her husband caught hold of her veil and said in a rage, "You light a fire in my heart and then just leave? Where are you going?"

Teeja told him gently, "What's the point of telling you when you won't listen to the truth?"

"The point? *I* am the one who decides what the point is. Where are you sneaking off to without my permission?"

How could an abyss so vast and deep have grown between them overnight? Teeja took care with her words as she explained, "You are just not your own self today. I was going over to see your cousin to see how she's getting along now. I'm sure you'll be back to your old self in a few weeks. I'll return as soon as you send word."

"What kind of cud are you trying to make me swallow? You want to band together with those spirits and do me in? I know when I see rand-whores like you. Go up to the bedroom right now or else…"

"Or else what?" Teeja teased, smiling all the while.

When he saw that smirk on Teeja's face, he completely lost control. He dropped her veil and grabbed her braid. She collapsed in a heap with a single tug. Then he dragged her by her hair, hissing, "I'm not any woman's slave that I'd be taken in by these wiles." He pulled Teeja into the bedroom and threw her down on the bed. Teeja ground her teeth and squeezed her eyes shut tight. She felt such a powerful aversion towards this man she wouldn't let even the slightest moan escape her lips. She was so frightened she couldn't breathe. Soon she felt her consciousness dipping beneath the surface, drowning in an unfathomable tunnel of darkness.

He left her there unconscious in the rang mahal and bolted the front door shut. Then he ran into the nearby jungle like a madman. Before long he had reached the same hillside that Beeja and Teeja had played upon that first afternoon together. It was just a big, shapeless pile of dry rocks now, ugly and discoloured. He felt as if all of nature were hanging her head in mourning.

When he reached the top of the hill, he remembered how it had been that day. He closed his eyes and that scene hovered before him. He opened his eyes again with a start. Where were those heavy clouds that threatened to send down wreaths of rain? Where was the drumming thunder? Where were those lips? Where was that naked embrace? Where was that unbroken gaze of love? Every hair on his body began yearning to become Beeja again. And as soon as the wish was made, his body began to change. Those same smooth cheeks as before. Her shirtfront tightened with the pressure of two lotuses blossoming underneath. They were impatient to feel the touch of Teeja's hand once more.

Beeja ran down the mountain as fast as she could, yanked open the bolts on the Ikthamba Mahal and ran inside. She hurried to the rang mahal and shook the unconscious Teeja, "Teeja!... Teeja!... I gave up my man's shell. Open your eyes and behold your old Beeja for yourself!"

She had to shake her and shake her with some force before Teeja finally returned to consciousness. As her eyelashes fluttered open, she saw her own Beeja hanging over her like a nagar-bel vine! Those eyes overflowing with love! That soft, scented body! They held each other in an embrace so tight, it hasn't slackened even after all these years.

And the spirit chief's miracles never cease: that loathsome seed of man planted in Teeja's womb was reduced to ash, along with the tender shoots growing there. After that no male of any species – even a bird – could go near the Ikthamba Mahal for twelve and twelve makes twenty four kos. Except once when Teeja invited the author there. He saw the Ikthamba Mahal with his own eyes and wrote what Teeja told him to write word for word. And we have passed on the tale in this language just as respectfully. If we have added even a single word to her tale, Lord Ram only knows what the spirit chief would do to us!

genealogy

English title	Hindi title	Rajasthani title	Previous source (oral, etc.)
Chouboli	—	Chouboli *Baatan ri Phulwari,* Vol. 8, p.177	Oral folktale — Savalram (Bhambi)
The Ninety-Nine Rupee Snare	Ninyanwe ka Pher *Uljhan*, p.28	Ninyanbe rau Pher *Baatan ri Phulwari*, Vol.4	Oral folktale— common (no one particular)
The Crafty Thief	Phitarti Chor *Uljhan*, p.80	Khantilou Chor *Baatan ri Phulwari*, Vol. 10, p.255	Oral folktale— Jagaram Singh
Weigh Your Options	Riayat *Duvidha*, p.175	Uchhal Panthi *Baatan ri Phulwari*, Vol.12, p.99	Kumbha Ram, a politician, who said this in his speech
The Dilemma	Duvidha *Duvidha*, p.249	Duvidhya *Baatan ri Phulwari*, Vol.10, p.172	Oral folktale for getting rid of a fever
I'm Alive I'm Awake	—	Mhai Jiyun Hoon Mhai Jaagun Hoon *Baatan ri Phulwari*, Vol. II, p.129	Oral folktale— Balu Bai (his sister-in-law)
Cannibal	Adamkhor *Uljhan*, p.61	Adamkhor *Baatan ri Phulwari*, Vol. 11, p.25	Oral folktale— Jagaram Singh
The Thakur's Ghost	Thakur ka Bhoot	Thakur rau Bhoot *Baatan ri Phulwari*, Vol. 9, p.205	Oral folktale— Bhola Ram (Ranava Rajput)
To Each Her Own	Apni-apni Khushbu *Duvidha*, p.31	Aap Apri Sourabh *Baatan ri Phulwari*, Vol. 13, p.73	Story in *The Gospel* *of Ramakrishna*
Alexander and the Crow	Sikander aur Kauwa *Sapnapriya*, p.266	—	Oral folktale— Chandra Prasad Deval

The Limit	Seema *Uljhan*, p.70	Math *Baatan ri Phulwari*, Vol. 11, p.44	Jagaram Singh
A Hound's Pride	Nahargarh *Uljhan*, p.50	Gindak valou Guman *Baatan ri Phulwari*, Vol.12, p.63	Elaboration of a kahavat
The Dove and the Snake	Kameri aur Saamp *Anokha Ped*	Kameri ar Sarap *Baatan ri Phulwari*, Vol. II, p.271	Oral folktale— Jagaram Singh
A Straw Epic	Trinbharat *Uljhan*, p.28	Trnbharat *Baatan ri Phulwari*, Vol. 13, p.107	Oral folktale— Jagaram Singh
Two Lives	Dohari Zindagi *Duvidha*, p.14	Dovari Joon *Lok Sanskriti*, 1975, p.5	Oral folktale— a Jain sadhu told the story while giving a bakhan, or religious teaching
Untold Hitlers	Anekhon Hitler *Duvidha*, p.14	Alekhun Hitler *Alekhun Hitler*, p.60	Story overheard on a bus (ostensibly true)
Press the Sap, Light the Lamp	Ras Kas Diya Jale *Phulwari*, p.45	Ras Kas Divlou Bale *Baatan ri Phulwari*, Vol. 10, p.1	Oral folktale— Jagaram Singh
A True Calling	Rijak ki Maryada *Kathadesh*, March 1997	Rijak ri Marjada *Baatan ri Phulwari*, Vol. 3	Oral folktale— Jatan Singh Rathour

Bibliography

Detha, Vijaydan. *Baatan ri Phulwari*. Borunda: Rupayan Sansthan, Vol. 1-14, 1960-1989.

Detha, Vijaydan. *Lok Sanskriti*. Borunda: Rupayan Sansthan, 1975.

Kabir, Kailash, trans. *Duvidha aur Anya Kahaniya*. New Delhi: Rajkamal Prakashan, 1979.

Kabir, Kailash, trans. *Uljhan*. New Delhi: Rajkamal Prakashan, 1982.

Detha, Vijaydan. *Alekhun Hitler*. New Delhi: Rajkamal Prakashan, 1984.

Detha, Vijaydan. *Sapnapriya*. New Delhi: Bharatiya Jnanpith, 1998.

Detha, Vijaydan. *Antaral*. Delhi: Janvani Prakashan, 1998.

bionotes

Vijaydan Detha's lively, wry, and irreverent folk-based tales have been widely read, loved, and awarded since the 1970s. One of the most prolific writers in Indian literature today, he has to his credit more than 800 short stories, which have been translated into Hindi, English and other languages. Bijji – as Detha is affectionately called – has a gift for selecting the most provocative tales he hears from his fellow villagers and recreating them in a literary form as engaging and as daring as his oral sources. His short fiction anthologies in Rajasthani include *Baatan Ri Phulwari, Alekhun Hitler, Roonkh* and *Kaboo Rani*; while *Anokha Ped, Antaral, Phoolwari* and *Priya Mrinal* are in Hindi. Other than his two novels *Uljhan* in Rajasthani and *Mahamilan* in Hindi, Detha has also written critical works including *Bapu Ke Teen Hatyare* and *Atirikta*, composed poetry, and edited several volumes of Rajasthani folklore and folk songs.

Apart from writing, this 82 year old resident of village Borunda, near Jodhpur, has also been working tirelessly for the Rupayan Sansthan, an institute that Detha established in 1960 with the late Komal Kothari. The Sansthan does archival and research work on various Indian folk art forms, folk music, folk ballads, folk epics, folk gods and goddesses, food, nomads and pastoral ways of life, ethno-geography; and finally on the ethno-mind – in trying to locate the traditional ways in which one generation passes its knowledge and skills to the next generation where the practice is to "learn but not teach" in any structural way.

Detha is a writer who makes brilliant use of Rajasthani folklore to highlight contemporary issues. In 2005, Katha honoured this teller of fine stories for his generous vision and inimitable style with the Katha Chudamani: a Lifetime Achievement Award rooted in Katha's belief that true art not only speaks of life but is also the source of the living truth; it manifests both creativity and daya – empathy for the living. Vijaydan Detha is testimony to this: his short stories and novels are desert-children, borne of the folk-landscape he inhabits. In his own words, "The stories of the desert are like its sand, fine and transparent." He is also the recipient of the Sahitya Akademi Award for Rajasthani, the Bhartiya Bhasha Parishad Award, the Sahitya Chudamani, and the Padma Shri.

Christi A Merrill is Assistant Professor of South Asian Literature and Postcolonial Theory at the University of Michigan. She translates postcolonial writing from Hindi, Rajasthani, and French, and writes on the practice and politics of translation. Her recently published work *Riddles of Belonging: India in Translation and Other Tales of Possession* extensively refers to Detha's works, among other Indian writers.

Kailash Kabir has translated much of Vijaydan Detha's works into Hindi. Primarily a poet, he has published a collection of Hindi poems titled *Tumhare Aane Par*. He has also translated A K Ramanujan's *Folktales of India* from English into Hindi. He is the recipient of the Sahitya Akademi National Award for Translation, as well as the Rajasthan Sahitya Akademi Award for Poetry.